To

From

Date

Bedtime
Devotions
with Jesus

MyDaily™
Devotional
for Kids

Tommy NELSON

A Division of Thomas Nelson Publishers
Since 1798

Bedtime Devotions with Jesus
MyDaily™ Devotional for Kids
© 2014 by Tommy Nelson

Published in Nashville, Tennessee, by Tommy Nelson. Tommy Nelson is an imprint of Thomas Nelson. Thomas Nelson is a registered trademark of HarperCollins Christian Publishing, Inc.

Thomas Nelson titles may be purchased in bulk for educational, business, fund-raising, or sales promotional use. For information, please e-mail SpecialMarkets@ThomasNelson.com.

Cover and interior design by Kristy L. Edwards.
Images copyright Mariia Sats / Shutterstock (www.shutterstock.com).

ISBN 978-0-7180-3645-4

Printed in China

16 17 18 19 DSC 11 10 9 8 7

www.thomasnelson.com

Train a child how to live the right way. Then even
when he is old, he will still live that way.
Proverbs 22:6

Dear Parents,

L ife is so busy today, for parents and children
alike. It is often a great challenge to find quiet
time every day to spend with God and His Word. This
52-week devotional will help you enjoy those moments
with your children as you teach them about the Lord
and what the Bible says about how we are supposed to
follow Him.

Each day contains a verse, a devotion, a prayer, and
a truth about God for your child to hold on to. Using
simple language and charming illustrations, this
collection offers children messages about telling the
truth, loving and trusting God with their whole heart,
doing the right thing even when no one is looking, and
so much more about following God.

In those quiet moments at night before your child
goes to sleep, snuggle up and share these daily
reminders of God's love and care, instilling His
teachings in your child's heart.

Contents

Forgive Like Jesus

"If your brother sins, tell him he is wrong. But if he is sorry and stops sinning, forgive him."

Luke 17:3

Is it wrong to be hurt and even mad when someone lies or takes your things or says something ugly to you? Of course not! Jesus says it is okay to tell someone that what she did was wrong. But He also says we should forgive that person when she says she is sorry. Jesus always forgives us, and so we should forgive too.

Dear Lord, You always forgive. Make me be more like You.

I want to forgive and be more like Jesus.

Forgive Again

"You must forgive him even if he does wrong to you 70 times 7."
Matthew 18:22

Your little sister has messed up your room . . . again. She feels really, really bad and says that she is sorry. But you are mad and do not really want to forgive her again. It is hard, but Jesus says no matter how many times someone does something wrong, when they say they are sorry, we should forgive them. Jesus has forgiven us for so much because He loves us. Ask Jesus to remind you of His forgiveness when you have done something wrong. Ask Him to help you forgive others as He forgave you.

Jesus, thank You for forgiving me when I do something wrong. Help me forgive others when they hurt me.

I am forgiven because Jesus forgives.

Love Forgives

Love forgives all wrongs.
Proverbs 10:12

When someone hurts us, we have a decision to make: do we get mad at them or do we love them? What would Jesus want us to do? God is love, and He always chooses to love us. When we love Jesus, we can love others, even the people who are sometimes unlovable. Ask Jesus to help you love and forgive.

Jesus, thank You for loving me when I am good and when I am bad. Help me act more like You.

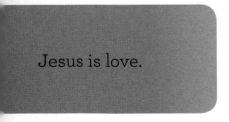

Jesus is love.

Dr. Johnny Hunt, First Baptist Woodstock, Woodstock, GA

Choose Forgiveness

"Forgive other people, and you will
be forgiven."

Luke 6:37

When your little brother breaks your favorite toy, what do you do? You might want to break his favorite toy so that he knows how you feel. But that is not what Jesus would do. Jesus would forgive your brother, and that is what you need to do. Forgiving others helps us be more like Jesus. The next time someone does something that makes you angry, choose to forgive!

Jesus, please help me be more like You, so that I may love others the way You love me.

Love is a choice and so is forgiveness.

Jesus Knows Us

Forgive the people and help them. Only you know what people are really thinking.

1 Kings 8:39

Jesus knows everything that you think and feel. You might be able to hide your feelings from your friends and family, but you cannot hide them from Jesus. Jesus knows all about us. Each morning, ask Jesus to be with you and help you love Him. You can talk to Jesus about anything, and He will be with you.

Jesus, help me remember today that You know the secrets of my heart.

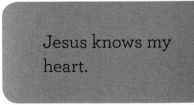

Jesus knows my heart.

Friends Forgive

Whoever forgives someone's sin
makes a friend.

Proverbs 17:9

It feels really good when a friend forgives us after we have done something bad. We can be friends again and have fun together. When your friend asks you to forgive him, remember how good it feels to be forgiven, and forgive your friend. Jesus is our best Friend, and He always forgives us when we do something wrong. Forgive your friends, and you will be more like Jesus.

Jesus, please help me be more like You and to forgive my friends.

Friends forgive
each other.

Love Jesus

"Love the Lord your God. Love him with all your heart, all your soul, all your mind, and all your strength."
Mark 12:30

Jesus wants us to love Him with our whole heart. He wants to be the most important thing in our lives. God has given us many wonderful things to enjoy. But the Bible tells us to love Jesus more than anything we have. Just like you can't have fun riding a bicycle if it only has one wheel, we can't love God the way He wants us to unless we love Him with all of our heart.

Jesus, I love You with all my heart. I want to love You more than anything You have given to me.

Jesus wants to be number one in my life.

Mrs. Janet Hunt, First Baptist Woodstock, Woodstock, GA

Live for Jesus

If we live, we are living for the Lord.
Romans 14:8

It is not always easy to share. Sometimes we just do not want to. But that does not make Jesus happy. He wants us to do what is right and share what we have with others. As children of God, we should think of other people and not just think of ourselves. It makes Jesus happy when we are kind and loving. You are the most like Jesus when you are giving and sharing.

Jesus, thank You for teaching me to give to others. I want to make You happy by being kind and sharing what I have.

Sharing shows we love Jesus.

Jesus Is Love

Lord, you are kind and forgiving.
You have great love for those who
call to you.

Psalm 86:5

Have you ever done something you knew was wrong? Did you tell the person you hurt that you were sorry? Did they forgive you? We should also tell Jesus that we are sorry when we have said or done something unkind. He likes for us to talk to Him. The Bible says Jesus will forgive us because He loves us.

Jesus, thank You for letting me talk to You.
Thank You for being kind and forgiving
when I do something wrong. Thank You
for loving me.

Jesus is kind,
forgiving, and loving.

Jesus Is Our Helper

Praise the Lord, day by day. God
our Savior helps us.

Psalm 68:19

Praising the Lord means telling Him how wonderful we think He is. We should praise Jesus and thank Him every day because He is always there for us. When we are scared, He is there. When we feel alone, He is there. When we feel sad, He is there. He never, ever leaves us. Sing a song to Jesus, and thank Him for being your helper whenever you need Him.

Jesus, thank You for always being there for me and for helping me when I need You most.

Sing songs of praise to Jesus, our helper.

Jesus Leads the Way

God has made Jesus both Lord and Christ.

Acts 2:36

Have you ever played "Follow the Leader"? One person is in charge, and whatever he does, you do it, too. Jesus is our leader. We should learn about Jesus and do what He does. The best way to know Jesus is to read God's Word, the Bible. Then you will know how to follow Him. The more you know about Jesus, the more you can be like Him.

Lord, help me read my Bible to know and do what is right so I can follow You.

Jesus will lead, and I will follow.

Do You Believe?

If you believe in your heart that God raised Jesus from death, then you will be saved.

Romans 10:9

When Jesus died on the cross, people thought He would never come back. But then a wonderful miracle happened! After lying dead for three days, Jesus got up and was alive again! All of Jesus' friends were so happy to see Him. Jesus is special because He is God's own Son. When you believe this in your heart, you can become part of God's family and live with Him in heaven some day.

Dear God, thank You for the miracle of Jesus being raised from the dead. Thank You that He is alive and can be a friend to us today.

Jesus is alive!

Masterpiece

You believers are like a building that God owns. . . . Christ Jesus himself is the most important stone in that building.

Ephesians 2:20

Do you like to build things? It is fun to see how tall you can make something with blocks or Legos. It is best to start building with the strongest and biggest pieces on the bottom. If you do not, your masterpiece will probably fall! The Bible tells us we should build our lives the same way. Make Jesus the most important part of your life. When Jesus comes first, everything you do will be better!

Dear Jesus, thank You for loving me, and help me always keep You as the most important part of my life.

Jesus should always be first in your heart.

The Maker of All

[Christ] is the head of the body. (The body is the church.) Everything comes from him.

Colossians 1:18

You cannot see inside your head, but your brain is working all the time. The brain is very important and controls your body. We cannot see God, but He controls the entire universe! God created the world and every living thing. God is the ruler over all. We should thank God every day for making us and the world we live in.

Dear God, I love the world You created. Thank You for making me. Help me follow You.

God is in charge of the whole world.

Be a Helper

I became a servant of the church because God gave me a special work to do that helps you.

Colossians 1:25

Have you thought about what you want to be when you grow up? Maybe you will be a police officer or a school teacher. You may even become a pastor or a missionary in a country far away. No matter what you decide to be, God has a special job for you. He wants you to tell others about Jesus and how much He loves them. Even now, you can help others and share Jesus' love with your friends and family.

Dear Jesus, thank You for my family and friends. Help me show Your love every day.

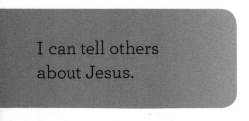

I can tell others about Jesus.

Praise the Lord

To him be glory in the church and in Christ Jesus for all time, forever and ever.

Ephesians 3:21

Have you ever had to go to a different school or move to a new house? Change is hard, and sometimes it is kind of scary. But one thing never changes: Jesus. He is always with us, and He will never leave us. Anytime of the day and anywhere we are, we can talk to God. We can pray to thank God for always being there, for taking care of us, and for loving us. We can sing songs that bring glory and praise to Jesus!

Dear Jesus, I love You. Thank You for loving me. I never want to forget to praise You.

Jesus will never stop loving you.

Grow Strong

No person ever hates his own body, but feeds and takes care of it. And that is what Christ does for the church.

Ephesians 5:29

Food is good for you. And it can taste very yummy! We need food to help our bodies grow and stay healthy. We need Jesus the same way. The Bible teaches us about Jesus and tells us how we should live. Learning about God's Word will make you wise and help you grow strong in Jesus.

Dear Jesus, thank You for the Bible. Help me grow big and strong and love You more every day.

Jesus takes care of you.

Show Gratitude

Now, brothers, we ask you to respect those people who work hard with you, who lead you in the Lord and teach you.

1 Thessalonians 5:12

Do you have a favorite teacher? Can you think of someone who helps you and is always kind? It might be a person at school, church, in your neighborhood, or in your family. Think of a way you can tell them or show them how thankful you are for them. Jesus puts special people in our lives to take care of us and teach us how to make good choices. Thank those special people for showing you God's love.

Dear Jesus, thank You for the special people You have put in my life who love me. Thank You for my family and friends. Help me follow You.

Jesus will show you how to follow Him.

Head, Heart, and Hands

Serve only the Lord your God. Respect him. Keep his commands and obey him. Serve him and be loyal to him.

Deuteronomy 13:4

God made every part of you! Look at your hands. What nice thing can you do for someone today? God gave you a brain to think. Who can you pray for today? God made your heart. Who can you show God's love to today? God gave you all of these parts to serve Him. Imagine all the things you can do with God and for God.

Dear Jesus, thank You for making me. Show me fun ways to serve you with my head, heart, and hands.

Serve God with your head, heart, and hands today!

Hollie Hixson, Vinings Lake Church, Mableton, GA

Better Than Any "Thing"

"You cannot serve God and money at the same time."

Matthew 6:24

What is your favorite toy? Are you careful so you don't break it? Do you keep it in a safe place? You probably take great care of it because you love it! Do you remember who gave you your special toy? Sometimes we let our things become more important than the one who gave them to us. God loves to give to us, but let's remember to love Him more than our things.

Thank You, Jesus, for giving me everything I need. Please help me not make anything more important than You.

Make God your favorite, and thank Him for every "thing" you have been given!

Love Jesus

That law is to love the Lord your God and obey his commands. Continue to follow him and serve him the very best you can.

Joshua 22:5

Have you ever disobeyed your parents? Your parents love you very much, and they want you to do what they say because they know what is best for you. Jesus wants us to obey Him too. He loves you more than you can imagine, and He always knows the right thing to do. We should obey Jesus and love Him because of His super-great love for us.

Dear Jesus, thank You for loving me. Please help me obey my parents and obey what the Bible teaches me.

Obeying my parents is one way I can show my love for God.

Happy Heart

Serve the Lord with joy. Come before him with singing.

Psalm 100:2

Do you like to sing? It is fun to sing songs that tell Jesus how much we love Him. He loves it when we share our happy heart with Him. So the next time you have a happy heart, sing a song and thank Jesus! That is serving God with joy. You can serve God with joy every day!

Dear Jesus, thank You for loving me and making my heart happy.

It makes Jesus happy when we sing a song of praise to Him.

God Never Changes

Remember that you will receive your reward from the Lord, which he promised to his people.

Colossians 3:24

G od keeps His promises, and He promises that He will always love you. No matter what you do, His love for you will never change. Isn't that awesome! Today, thank God for always loving you, and think of some ways that you can show God how much you love Him too!

Dear Jesus, thank You for loving me. I love You.

I get to love God because He loves me!

Hollie Hixson, Vinings Lake Church, Mableton, GA

All the Pieces

Serve the Lord with all your heart.
1 Samuel 12:20

What if someone gave you a puzzle but it didn't have all the pieces? You wouldn't be able to put the whole picture together. Sometimes we let other things be more important than God. But God wants us to love Him with all of our heart. He wants to be the most important person in our life. Pray to God today and ask Him to help you always put Him first.

Dear Jesus, please help me love You with all of my heart today.

Love God with all your heart.

The Greatest Gift

"For God loved the world so much that he gave his only Son. God gave his Son so that whoever believes in him may not be lost, but have eternal life."

John 3:16

Do you know how much God loves you? He loves you so much that He gave you a very important gift. God sent His Son to die for your sins on the cross. He is willing to forgive every bad thing you do if you will believe in Him. Thank God for the best gift you will ever get, and love God with all your heart.

Jesus, thank You for sending Your Son to earth to show me how much You love me. I believe in You and will live my life for You.

There is no greater gift than Jesus.

When You Make Mistakes

But Christ died for us while we were still sinners. In this way God shows his great love for us.

Romans 5:8

The Bible calls the bad things we do, like disobeying our parents, telling a lie, or saying mean things, sins. The good news is that God loves us even when we make bad choices. Nothing you do, no matter how bad, will ever change how much Jesus loves you. He died on the cross for your sins and wants to forgive you.

Jesus, thank You for loving me even when I misbehave. Please forgive me for disobeying You. I love You.

> Jesus loves me so much that He died for me.

God's Special Promise for You

I love those who love me. Those who want me find me.

Proverbs 8:17

What is wisdom and why do you need it? Wisdom is understanding the world the way God wants you to. When you look for God and want His wisdom, He promises to give it to you. That is why reading your Bible, going to church, and learning about God from others is so important. God loves when people want to know Him and what He says. If you ask God to help you learn more about Him each day, He promises to answer.

Jesus, I want to be wise. Help me love You enough to learn all I need to know.

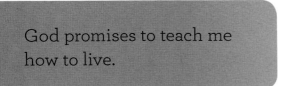

God promises to teach me how to live.

Showing God's Love to Others

God is love. Whoever lives in love
lives in God, and God lives in him.
1 John 4:16

D o you want to be like God? Do you want
people to know that you love Him? If you
do, becoming a person who loves others is very
important. God is so loving that the Bible says He
is love. Loving others shows them what God is
like. It also shows that God is with us and that we
belong to Him. What are some things you can do to
love people the way God does?

Jesus, help me love others the way
You want me to. Help others feel Your
love because of the way I treat them.

God loves people
through me.

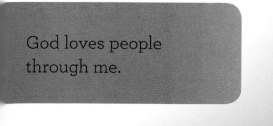

How Can I Show God I Love Him?

"I loved you as the Father loved me. Now remain in my love."

John 15:9

What does it mean to remain in God's love? How can we show Him how glad we are that He loves us? The answer is to obey Him. Jesus always did what God told Him to do because He loved His Father so much. When you obey your parents, you show them that you love them too. The same is true about God. Obeying God's commandments is like saying, "I love You!" to God. Name some things the Bible says we should do.

Jesus, I want to love You more every day. Help me remain in Your love by obeying what the Bible teaches.

My obedience shows God I love Him.

Love Others the Way God Loves You

"This is my command: Love each other as I have loved you."

John 15:12

What does it mean to love others the way God loves you? What are some things that Jesus did for us that we can do for others? Make sure you always tell people the truth. Notice those who do not seem to have any friends. Do kind things for others. Love those who are not nice to you. Pray for people who are hurting. Jesus did all these things for us. You can love others by following His example.

Jesus, thank You for showing me Your love. Help me do the same for others. Love people through me.

I can be like Jesus by loving others.

The Greatest Treasure Hunt

"The Son of Man came to find lost people and save them."

Luke 19:10

Have you ever lost something that was really important to you? You probably looked everywhere until you found your missing toy. God loves His people. He does not want them to ever be lost and not be with Him. So He sent His Son, Jesus, whom the Bible sometimes calls the Son of Man, to earth to save us all. It was the biggest treasure hunt ever. The treasure is you and me and people all over the world. Jesus came to earth to find us. Jesus came to save us.

Jesus, thank You for coming to earth to save me. Without You, I would be lost.

Jesus came to earth to find me and save me.

Dr. Alex Himaya, thechurch.at, Tulsa, OK

And That's the Truth!

"I tell you the truth. He who believes has eternal life."

John 6:47

We should always tell the truth. Jesus did. And He said that if you believe in Him, you get to live with Him forever and ever in heaven. That's what eternal life means. Eternal life is life that goes and on and on and on for infinity and beyond! When Jesus speaks, every word He says is true. You can believe Jesus every time!

Jesus, thank You for always telling the truth. I believe You. Thank You for forever and ever life.

Jesus always tells the truth.

Jesus Is the Super-est

> "We know that this man really is the Savior of the world."
>
> John 4:42

Who is your favorite superhero? Does he or she have special powers that they use to rescue people? Jesus is more amazing than the most amazing superhero. Jesus is God, and He came to earth to save the whole world! God is big and powerful, but He is also kind and gentle. God wants to save you right now! Believe in Jesus and He will save you.

Jesus, You are the super-est of superheroes. You are better than any superhero. You are the Savior of the world! I believe You will save me.

Jesus is the super-est of superheroes.

Who Do You See?

We have seen that the Father sent his Son to be the Savior of the world.

1 John 4:14

God in heaven is our forever Father. He had a plan to save the world, so He sent His Son, Jesus, to earth to be our Savior. Sin is the bad stuff that we do, and it has to be punished. Jesus loves us so much that He took the punishment for us. Now we can be with Jesus and God in heaven.

Jesus, thank You for coming to earth to take my punishment and save me.

When I look at Jesus, I see God's love.

Happy Heart Dance Song

"My soul praises the Lord; my heart is happy because God is my Savior."
Luke 1:46–47

Praising is the same thing as saying, "You are awesome!" or "What you did was so cool!" God loves it when we tell Him how much we love Him. One of the ways we tell God that we think He is wonderful is by singing songs to Him. Jesus came to save us. And that should make us very happy! Sing a song to God today and thank Him for loving you and saving you. Your heart will be happy when you are praising God.

Jesus, You make my heart feel good. You found me and saved me. I love to tell You, "Thank You!"

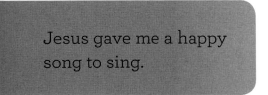

Jesus gave me a happy song to sing.

Dr. Alex Himaya, thechurch.at, Tulsa, OK

Have Mercy!

He saved us because of his mercy,
not because of good deeds we did to
be right with God.

Titus 3:5

Good deeds are things like picking up your toys
or eating all of your dinner. It is important
to obey your parents and do the right things. But
doing those things does not get you into heaven.
We get to go to heaven when we love Jesus. Jesus
loves us so much that He came to earth to save us.
Good deeds will not make us right with God. Jesus
makes us right with God. Jesus puts you, me, and
God back together.

Jesus, You saved me because You
are kind and giving. I want to do good
things, but it is Your love that saves me.

Jesus makes us right
with God.

Trust Jesus

You give peace to those who depend on you. You give peace to those who trust you.

Isaiah 26:3

Babies cannot take care of themselves. Someone has to feed them and dress them. They need someone to give them a bath. They even need someone to carry them around. Babies depend on their parents to take care of them. You trust and depend on your parents too. They make your meals. They help you when you are sad or hurt. You can also trust and depend on Jesus. He watches over you. You can be peaceful, just like a sleeping baby, when you trust that Jesus is always there for you.

Help me trust You, Jesus, so I can have peace.

Trusting Jesus brings peace.

Jesus Gives Peace

Lord, all our success is because of what you have done. So give us peace.

Isaiah 26:12

You have many people who love you. Your family loves you. Your friends love you. Your teachers care about you. And Jesus loves you. Jesus cares so much about you that He did something amazing. He died on the cross and rose again so you can be part of God's family. When you believe that Jesus died to pay for your sins, you can have peace with God.

Jesus, thank You for helping me be part of God's family. Help me remember that You always love me.

Jesus has taken care of everything!

Picture This

The God who gives peace will be
with you.

Philippians 4:9

I t is fun to think about things that make you
happy. Think about a special time you had with
your family. Now think about your favorite book
or toy. Thinking about God is fun too. God made
everything in the world. He even made you. God
wants you to remember Him when you see the
things He made. What is something God made
that makes you happy? The next time you see that
thing, remember that God made it and that He
loves you.

Jesus, thank You for making everything. Thank You that
I can see what You made to remind me that You love me.

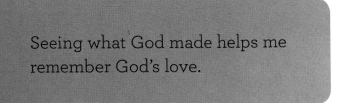

Seeing what God made helps me
remember God's love.

Dan and Debbie Kubish, NewSpring Church, Wichita, KS

Good Night, Sleep Tight

I go to bed and sleep in peace. Lord, only you keep me safe.

Psalm 4:8

Sam was afraid to go to bed. At bedtime, he asked his mom for a story. Then he asked for a drink. Then he asked for a hug. He didn't want his mom to leave the room because he was scared when he was by himself. His night light made a big shadow on the wall. The wind made weird sounds. Mom showed Psalm 4:8 to Sam. It says that Jesus is always with him to keep him safe, even at night.

Jesus, help me go to sleep because I know You are keeping me safe.

Jesus is bigger than my fear!

Don't Worry

"My peace I give you. . . . So don't let your hearts be troubled. Don't be afraid."

John 14:27

One day Jesus was talking with His friends. He told them that He would be going away soon. He had an important job to do, but they did not understand. They wanted to go with Him. They were afraid. Jesus told them not to be afraid. He told them that He would give them peace so they would not need to worry. Jesus can take care of everything we need. We do not need to worry either.

Jesus, I am scared sometimes. Please help me remember that You will take care of everything.

When I feel afraid, I will tell Jesus.

Think Peace

Let the peace that Christ gives
control your thinking.

Colossians 3:15

Pretend you have a big empty bucket. When you
pick it up, it feels light. Then someone puts a
brick in it. Later someone else puts another brick
in it. Then you put a brick in it. At the end of the
day, your bucket is very heavy. It is hard to carry.
The bricks are like bad thoughts. Sometimes bad
or mean thoughts come in our heads and upset us.
They make us feel like we are carrying a bucket of
bricks. Instead, think about Jesus and His love. He
brings peace and makes your bucket light again.

Jesus, help me think about You so I can have a
peaceful day.

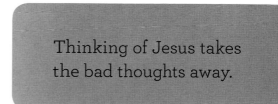

Thinking of Jesus takes
the bad thoughts away.

Friends Forever

"I stand at the door and knock. If anyone hears my voice and opens the door, I will come in."

Revelation 3:20

Have you ever invited some friends over to play? Remember how excited you were while you waited for them to get there? When they finally knocked on the door, what did you do? You probably opened the door and let them come in. Jesus wants to come over and spend time with you too. The best part is that Jesus never has to leave and go home.

Jesus, I am so excited that You want to spend time with me. Thanks for being my forever friend.

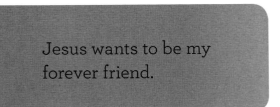

Jesus wants to be my forever friend.

Anne Chenault, First Baptist Church, Chipley, FL

Honest Friends

The Lord . . . is a friend to those
who are honest.

Proverbs 3:32

Have you ever wanted a best friend? What kind of friend were you looking for? Do you know that God wants friends too? The Bible says God is a friend to people who are honest. God looks for friends who tell the truth. Remember to pick friends like Jesus did. Choose kids that tell the truth. Make sure you tell the truth, too, so people will want to be your friend.

Dear Jesus, I want to be Your friend. Please help me always tell the truth, even when it is hard. Help me choose honest friends.

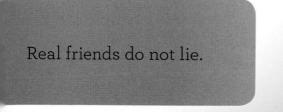

Real friends do not lie.

The Best Friend

"I don't call you servants. . . . But now I call you friends because I have made known to you everything I heard from my Father."

John 15:15

Jesus says He is our friend. He proved it by telling us everything He knows about His Father, God. Tell your friends about God so that they can be friends with Him too.

Dear Jesus, thank You for being my very best friend. Help me know how to tell my friends about God.

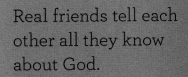

Real friends tell each other all they know about God.

Being Friends
with Jesus

"You are my friends if you do what I
command you."

John 15:14

D o you want to be friends with Jesus? The Bible
says that if you want to be friends with Jesus,
you have to love Him and do what He says. If you
want to learn about Jesus, you can find out about
Him in your Bible. Read your Bible every day or get
someone to read it to you. Then you will know how
to be best friends with Jesus.

Jesus, I want us to be friends. Help me learn about You
and do the things that make You happy.

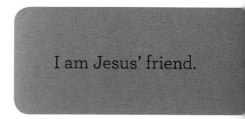

I am Jesus' friend.

What Real Friends Do

Come near to God, and God will come near to you.

James 4:8

You have a special invitation. It is from God Himself! He is inviting you to come and spend time with Him. You can sing songs to God, learn about Him in your Bible, and talk to Him in your prayers. The more time you spend together, the better friends you will become. God loves spending time with His friends.

Jesus, I want to spend time with You every day. I want us to become the best of friends. Thanks for inviting me.

Real friends spend time together.

Anne Chenault, First Baptist Church, Chipley, FL

Fun Times with Friends

The fellowship we share together is with God the Father and his Son, Jesus Christ.

1 John 1:3

Why is spending time with friends so much fun? The Bible says that the fun times you share together are so good because you share them with God and Jesus. When you and your friends get together, remember God and Jesus are there also. You can thank Him for the sunshine or the mud puddles. You can sing to Him as you swing as high as His clouds. Remember to include God and Jesus, and then times spent with friends get even better.

Jesus, thanks so much for my friends and the fun times we share together.

Fun times are best when shared with friends.

Together with Jesus

It is God who has made you part of Christ Jesus.

1 Corinthians 1:30

Have you watched your mom or dad make Kool-Aid? They took the packet of flavoring and poured it into a container of water. Then they stirred the flavoring and water together and it made Kool-Aid! Two things actually became one.

That's what happens when Jesus becomes our Savior. We become part of Him, and nothing can ever separate us from Him.

Father, thank You that You will always stay with me. Help me remember that for the rest of my life.

Jesus will live with me forever.

My Sin Eraser

Christ is the reason we are right
with God and have freedom.

1 Corinthians 1:30

Why do you think pencils have erasers?
Because we make mistakes, right? We
all need erasers. The Bible says that we all make
mistakes. We don't always do the right thing.
God is sad when that happens. When you make a
mistake, say, "I am sorry, God." Jesus hears you
and asks God to forgive you. God always listens to
His Son. Jesus is the eraser that fixes our mistakes
when we ask Him to.

Jesus, thank You for forgiving me when I am wrong. I
want to make You happy in everything I do.

Jesus talks to God
for me.

I Believe Because

God makes people right with himself
through their faith in Jesus Christ.
Romans 3:22

G od always tells the truth all the time. He said
in the Bible that if you believe in His Son,
Jesus, He will always be with you. God wants you
to be with Him because He loves you. He will
always do what He says He will do, so you can trust
that He is with you. He is your friend forever.

God, thank You for sending Your Son so that He could
be my friend.

Jesus is God's Son
and my friend.

Dr. Mike Whitson, First Baptist Church, Indian Trail, NC

Jesus Is Within Me

If Christ is in you, then the Spirit gives you life, because Christ made you right with God.

Romans 8:10

D o you like blowing bubbles? You put the stick in the liquid, hold it up, blow gently, and the bubble is formed. Your breath is inside the bubble. When you ask Jesus to come into your life, you become like that bubble. He comes into your life, and suddenly you have Jesus inside you. Thank Jesus today for always being with you.

God, thank You for the joy of knowing Jesus. I am glad that joy will never leave me.

Jesus makes me bubble over with joy.

Who Am I Like?

But then the kindness and love of
God our Savior was shown.

Titus 3:4

Jesus was the kindest man who ever lived. The Bible says that He healed people when they were sick and comforted them when they were sad. Two times He gave enough food to feed hungry people. He made people feel good everywhere He went. How can you be more like Him? Do you know someone who is sad? Maybe you could make them happy by sharing a toy with them. Jesus said we should love everyone. That's what Jesus did.

God, help me share and love my friends and family. I want to show everyone that I love You.

I am like Jesus
when I love.

Believing Is Seeing

We believe with our hearts, and so
we are made right with God.

Romans 10:10

We have never seen God's face, but we know that He is with us. We can feel Him in our heart. God loves us so much that He sent His Son, Jesus, to die on the cross for our sins. Ask Jesus to forgive you for the wrong things you have done and to be your friend forever.

Father, even though I cannot see You, I believe the Bible is true. Please forgive me for all the wrong things I have done. I love You.

I believe the Bible is true.

God's Family

Jesus answered them, "My mother and my brothers are those who listen to God's teaching and obey it!"
Luke 8:21

H as your mom or dad ever asked you to do something? Did you listen to what they said and do what they asked? That is called obedience. The Bible teaches us that Jesus had a family. He had a mom, a dad, and even brothers. The Bible says that we can be a part of His family too. We are His family when we listen to *and* obey God.

Dear God, help me listen to You and obey what You say. Thank You for wanting me to be a part of Your family.

Think of one thing the Bible says that you can listen to and obey today.

Paul and Kimberly Purvis,
First Baptist Church Temple Terrace, Temple Terrace, FL

God Is Proud of You

[Jesus] is not ashamed to call them
his brothers.

Hebrews 2:11

God loves you so much that He wants the whole
world to know you are part of His family.
In fact, God is proud of you! Since God is not
ashamed of us, we should not be ashamed of Him.
We should tell everyone we know that we love
Jesus.

Thank You, God, for loving me. Help me tell others how
much I love You.

Tell somebody how much
you love God today.

You Get to Do This

But some people did accept him. They believed in him. To them he gave the right to become children of God.

John 1:12

C an you think of a time when you got to do something very special? Think about how that made you feel. The Bible says those who believe Jesus get to do something very special. They get to become a part of God's family. You are God's child when you accept Jesus and believe in Him. And that will make you feel great!

Dear Jesus, thank You for letting me be a part of God's family.

Tell somebody why you are glad you get to be part of God's family.

God Knows Your Name

The Father has loved us so much!
He loved us so much that we are
called children of God.

1 John 3:1

Jesus loves you so much that He gives you a special name. He calls you His child. That is amazing! You are a child of God! Because God loves you as one of His children, He takes special care of you. He listens to you, He helps you, and He is always with you. Imagine God calling your name right now. Then listen as He says, "You are mine!"

Thank You, God, for loving me so much. Thank You for watching out for me as Your child.

Tell somebody, "I am a child of God!"

Paul and Kimberly Purvis,
First Baptist Church Temple Terrace, Temple Terrace, FL

God Knew You First

God knew them before he made the world. And God decided that they would be like his Son. Then Jesus would be the firstborn of many brothers.

Romans 8:29

One of the greatest things about God is that He knows everything. Did you know that God knew He would make you before He made the whole world? That is how special you are to Him.

God also knew He wanted you to be a part of His family. Before God made the world, He knew He would send Jesus to love you. God loves you so much!

Thank You, God, for loving me even before You made the world. I love You too!

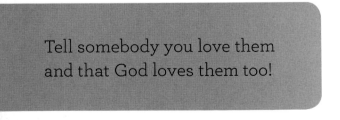

Tell somebody you love them and that God loves them too!

Paul and Kimberly Purvis,
First Baptist Church Temple Terrace, Temple Terrace, FL

Led by God's Spirit

The true children of God are those
who let God's Spirit lead them.

Romans 8:14

The Bible says God is our leader, and we should
always follow Him. When we follow Jesus,
we do what He says to do. God is always with us,
and His Spirit is always guiding us to make good
choices. Every day we have to decide: am I going
to do what I want to do, or am I going to follow my
leader?

Dear Jesus, help me follow You today.

Listen to Jesus and
follow Him.

The Best for You

Jesus answered, "If anyone loves me, then he will obey my teaching."
John 14:23

Jesus taught us a lot of things. He taught us to always tell the truth, even when it is not easy. He taught us to be nice to others, even when they are mean to us. Some of the things He taught are not always easy to do, but everything Jesus taught was to protect us and help us have a good life. Jesus loves you so much that He wants you to live the most incredible, best life ever.

Jesus, thank You for protecting me and for teaching me how to live the best life. Help me obey You, even when it is not easy.

Jesus wants the best for you.

I Promise

"Shout and be glad, Jerusalem. I am coming, and I will live among you," says the Lord.

Zechariah 2:10

God always keeps His promises. God promised that He would come and live with His people, and Jesus came to keep that promise. God said that no matter what happens, or how bad things look, He will help you and take care of you. Even when a situation seems scary, God is still in control and will keep His promise. So anytime you are scared or something bad is happening, remember that God always keeps His promises. He is with you!

Jesus, thank You for promising to take care of me. Help me remember that You always keep Your promises.

Jesus always keeps His promises.

Always There

> "This is true because if two or three people come together in my name, I am there with them."
>
> Matthew 18:20

Jesus is always with you. When you hear a noise at night and you do not know what it is, Jesus is with you. When someone says something mean to you and hurts your feelings, Jesus is with you. When you feel sad and alone, Jesus is with you! Jesus promised to never leave you, and Jesus always keeps His promises. So the next time you feel alone, hurt, or scared, remember that Jesus is with you and you can always talk to Him.

Jesus, thank You for being with me when I am scared, when I am alone, and when I am hurt. Because of You, I never have to face anything alone!

Jesus is always with you.

Ryan Hartzell, Hawk Creek Church, London, KY

God's Love

"He who knows my commands and obeys them is the one who loves me. And my Father will love him who loves me."
John 14:21

Jesus promises that God loves those who love Jesus. When we love someone, we spend time with them. God wants us to spend time with Jesus. When you talk to Jesus and read about Him in the Bible, you show Jesus that you love Him. You can trust everything that Jesus says because He loves you and will always protect you and watch over you. God loves you, He made you, and He wants the best for you! We can trust God because He loves us.

God, thank You for loving me. Help me trust You, listen to You, and do what You say.

I can trust God because He loves me.

The Light

Here is the message we have heard
from God and now tell to you:
God is light, and in him there is no
darkness at all.

1 John 1:5

The dark can be scary. But a lot of things that seem scary at night are not so scary when the sun comes up in the morning. The monster you thought you saw turns out to be a toy, or the scary shadow was just a tree branch outside your window. God is a lot like the sun. He helps us realize that things are not so scary. In fact, because of God, we have nothing to fear!

God, help me remember that I have nothing to fear because You are bigger than any problem.

Because of God, there is nothing to fear.

The Greatest Gift

God is faithful. He is the One who
has called you to share life with his
Son, Jesus Christ our Lord.

1 Corinthians 1:9

J esus loves you so much that He wants the
absolute best for you! In fact, He wants you to
be a part of His family. But there is a problem. It is
called sin. Sin is when we do what God tells us not
to do. Because of sin, we cannot be a part of God's
family. That is why Jesus came, lived a perfect life,
and died to pay for our sins, all so we could be a
part of God's family. Jesus loves you so much He
gave His life so you could live forever with Him in
heaven!

Jesus, thank You for giving Your life for me so that I can
live forever with You in heaven!

Jesus loves me so much
He gave His life for me.

Ryan Hartzell, Hawk Creek Church, London, KY   67

You Are in Good Hands

The everlasting God is your place of safety. His arms will hold you up forever.
Deuteronomy 33:27

Dad handed Gideon his baby sister. "Be careful with her, son. Do not drop Sophia. She is only two months old." After a minute, Gideon told his dad, "I am afraid. I cannot hold her any longer. You take her."

Sophia may have been too heavy for her small brother, but her dad had big hands and strong arms. Our God is our heavenly Father, and He carries us in His strong and loving arms. He will never drop us. We are in good hands.

Dear God, You are so strong, so big, and so mighty. Thank You for always holding on to me. I am safe in Your arms.

Jesus hugs me close to Him.

Safe!

*My God is my rock. I can run to
him for safety.*

2 Samuel 22:3

Have you ever played tag? If anyone gets
tagged, he is out of the game. The only way
to keep from getting out is to be holding on to the
place that has been called "safe." Michael was "it,"
so he ran to try to tag his cousins. Just as Michael
was about to tag him, Judah grabbed hold of the
big rock and said, "Safe." It is such a nice feeling to
know that nothing can happen to you because you
are safe. God is the safe place for you and me. He
will never, ever let us go.

Dear Lord, thank You that I have
someone to run to when I am afraid
and You will keep me safe.

Anyone holding on
to the Rock is safe!

I Am Inside the Safe

The Lord will be a safe place for his people.

Joel 3:16

Some people keep their most valuable stuff inside a special box or room that is called a *safe*. A safe can be made out of steel or concrete. It is called a safe because no one can rob or hurt anything that is inside. The Bible tells us that God is a safe place for you. No one can hurt you or take you away from Him. God will protect you. You are safe.

Dear Lord, thank You for taking such good care of me and keeping me safe.

The safest place in the world is with God.

A Shelter in the Storm

You are my protection, my place of safety in times of trouble.

Psalm 59:16

The clouds were big and rolling. Even though it was still daytime, the sky was getting dark. Silas watched the lightning come out of the clouds. He could hear thunder, but even though he was just six, he was not afraid because he was inside a storm shelter. That shelter was made to keep people safe from all kinds of storms. His mom and dad were in the shelter too. Did you know that God is a shelter for us? When things are happening around us that look scary, we do not have to be afraid. God will protect us and our family.

Dear Lord Jesus, thank You for always protecting me. I love You. I am not afraid because You keep me safe.

When something scares you, run to Jesus!

Dr. Michael Cloer, Englewood Baptist Church, Rocky Mount, NC   71

My Lifeguard

He took me to a safe place. Because
he delights in me, he saved me.

Psalm 18:19

Lifeguards are our friends. They help keep us
safe when we go to the beach. One day, a big
wave knocked Mary off her feet. In a moment,
Mary was out of sight. The water was over her head.
A lifeguard was watching and he immediately dove
in the water. In less than a minute, he had saved
Mary. She was now safe. Did you know God is
always watching you? He keeps you safe because
He loves you.

Dear Father, thank you for always being there for me.
I do not have to be afraid because I know You love me and
will save me when I call on You.

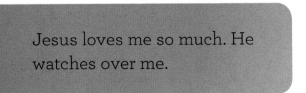

Jesus loves me so much. He
watches over me.

My Favorite Place

Be my place of safety where I can
always come.

Psalm 71:3

This is a big world. Sometimes it can be scary.
There are tall buildings and lots of people. At
times we can hear so much noise and have so many
things happening around us that we can be afraid.
Where do you want to go when you are scared?
Home is a safe place to go when you are frightened.
People are there who know you and care for you.
God wants you to come to Him when
you are afraid. He loves you, and
you are always safe with Him.

Dear Jesus, thank You for
loving me. Help me remember to
come to You when I am afraid.

I am always welcome
to come to God.

I Am Happy

Happy are the people whose God is the Lord.

Psalm 144:15

What makes you happy? How do you show that you are happy? Is it with a smile or a shout, or do you clap your hands? Our parents, our friends, and our favorite things can all make us happy. God says that people who love Him are happy. Even when bad things happen, we can be happy because we know that God is always with us. He loves us and takes care of us. It makes us happy to know that God loves us and is our friend.

Thank You, God, for loving my family and me. Help us love You every day and show other people we love you.

God loves me, and I am happy when I love Him back!

Truth Is Important

Happy is the person who finds
wisdom. And happy is the person
who gets understanding.

Proverbs 3:13

The proverbs were written so you can know God. We need to know what the Bible says so that we can learn about God and what He wants us to do. Do your parents or teachers give you instructions on how to do your schoolwork or clean your room? That's what Proverbs does. It tells us what we should do to follow God. We are happy if we know God and understand His Word. When we learn what He says, we know what to do. He always loves us and wants the best for us.

God, help me learn Your Word and follow Your instructions every day.

When we know what God
says, we know what to do.

I Will Follow

Those who obey what they have
been taught are happy.

Proverbs 29:18

God says it is important to obey Him. We know what God wants us to do when we read the Bible. If we ask for help to know what is right and wrong, then we will know how He wants us to live. People who do not follow God's Word end up doing the wrong things and get into trouble. God can only speak the truth. So what He tells us in the Bible is right and true. God says that He protects those who are honest and follow His way. When we listen to His Word and do what it says, we are obeying God. He says that when we know Him and follow Him, we will be happy.

God, thank You for the Bible and that it is true. Help my family and me happily follow what the Bible says.

God loves me so much that
He tells me the truth.

Pam Mercer, First Baptist Oviedo, Oviedo, FL

Doing the Right Thing

A person is blessed if he can do what he thinks is right without feeling guilty.
Romans 14:22

Do you feel happy when you do something good for someone else? It is so much fun to see other people happy. We should always try to do the right thing and follow God. Does that mean that everything will always turn out the way we want it to? No. Sometimes things are just hard. But when we do the right thing even when it is hard, God will be with us and protect us. The Bible says that we are happy when we do what is right.

God, please show me ways that I can do right and then help me do them.

We are happiest when we do what is right.

Trusting God

Whoever pays attention to what he is taught will succeed. And whoever trusts the Lord will be happy.

Proverbs 16:20

You may think that you are too young to hear what God says. But you are not! No matter how young or old you are, you can trust in God. If there is something you do not understand about trusting God, then you should ask your parents, your pastor, or your Sunday school teacher to help you. When we trust God, believe He tells the truth, and follow Him, we will be happy.

Dear God, help me learn more about You so I can trust You more. I trust You because I know You love me and tell the truth.

You are never too young to hear from God.

Being Kind

It is a sin to hate your neighbor.
But being kind to the needy brings
happiness.

Proverbs 14:21

Have you ever seen someone who needs help?
There are people in the world who do not
have food or a home. Sometimes people do not pay
attention to them and would rather they just go
away. But God loves them just like He loves us, and
He wants us to be kind to them. Maybe you have
a lot of toys, and you could ask your parents to
give some away to someone who doesn't have any.
When we do things for others, it makes God happy,
and it makes us happy too.

God, help those who need things and help me be kind to
others. Thank You for all You have given me.

Be kind to everyone!

A Father Cares

God is the Father who is full of
mercy [and] . . . all comfort.

2 Corinthians 1:3

Just like your mom or dad comforts you when you are hurt, Jesus is always there for you. When you learned to ride your bike, someone held the bike and ran beside you. You pedaled hard, and soon you could ride alone. There was probably a day when you fell off your bike and scraped your knee. Who made you feel better? Your mom or dad probably dried your tears and gave you a hug. When you are hurt, you can talk to Jesus. Jesus wants to make you feel better.

Thank You, God, that I can tell You when I am hurt. You love me and want me to feel better.

Talk to Jesus. He wants to comfort you.

Dr. Melissa Ewing, First Baptist Church McKinney, McKinney, TX

God Knows
Your Name

Does your life in Christ give you
strength? Does his love comfort you?
Philippians 2:1

*J*esus loves me, this I know, for the Bible tells me
so. This song reminds you that Jesus always
loves you. He never leaves you. He is always there.
You can feel safe knowing that God will be with
you wherever you go. He knows your name, and the
Bible says that He even knows the number of hairs
on your head. When you feel scared, remember
that God loves you. You can be strong
because He will never leave you alone.

Thank You, God, that You know my
name. Thank You that you never leave
me. Thank You for Your love.

You can feel safe because
God never leaves you alone.

Share Some Kindness

Jesus died for us so that we can live together with him. . . . So comfort each other and give each other strength.

1 Thessalonians 5:10–11

God wants you to be a good friend. Sometimes a kind word or friendly smile can make another person's day better. Do something nice for someone today. Make cookies for a neighbor who is sad. Invite a new kid at school to play with you during recess. When you are kind, you show the love of Jesus to another person. Can you make someone else feel happier today?

Thank You, God, for good friends. Help me be a good friend. Help me share Your love with someone else today.

Be kind and share Jesus' love with a friend.

Be Careful What You Say

We pray that the Lord Jesus Christ himself and God our Father will comfort you and strengthen you in every good thing you do and say.

2 Thessalonians 2:16

S ticks and stones may break your bones, but words will never hurt you. How untrue! Words can hurt. When you hurt someone's feelings, you can say, "I'm sorry." The Bible reminds us to use words of kindness and love. Psalm 19:14 says, "I hope my words and thoughts please you." God is happy when you say good things to someone else. Share the best words today and tell a friend, "Jesus loves you!"

Help me, God, to say I'm sorry when I do something wrong. Thank You for reminding me that my words are important.

Obey God and use kind words.

God Is Never Too Busy

God comforts those who are troubled.

2 Corinthians 7:6

When you are feeling sad, what makes you feel better? Sometimes the simplest things can change sadness into joy. A big, fuzzy blanket can make you feel cozy and warm on a cold winter day. Hugging a wiggly puppy can make you laugh. God gives us good things to enjoy. When you are sad, God will hear you when you pray. You can talk to God and tell Him how you feel. God is never too busy to listen. He cares for you.

Thank You, God, that I can tell You how I feel. I am glad You are never too busy for me.

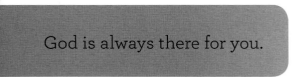

God is always there for you.

Do Not Worry About Anything

The Lord says, "I am the one who comforts you."

Isaiah 51:12

God cares about you. He helps you feel calm when you are worried. What makes you worry? When your mom leaves you with a babysitter, do you wonder when she will be home? On the first day of school, do you worry if you will like your teacher? Philippians 4:6 says, "Do not worry about anything. But pray and ask God for everything you need." God does not want you to worry. He wants you to talk to Him, and He will help you feel better.

Thank You, God, that I can talk to You when I am worried. Thank You for helping me feel calm.

Do not worry. God is with you.

Be Strong!

But, Lord, you are my shield. You are my wonderful God who gives me courage.

Psalm 3:3

Who is the strongest person you know? Is it Dad? Is it Mom? Is it a friend? God is the strongest person in the entire world. He is stronger than everyone else. There is no one like God. He is so strong that He protects you all the time. He is so strong that He takes care of you every day. Remember this and you can be brave all the time. Be strong!

Dear Lord, You are strong and take care of me. Help me know You are always with me.

Be brave because God is with you.

God Is Looking at You

"The Lord searches all the earth for people who have given themselves completely to him. He wants to make them strong."

2 Chronicles 16:9

Look up at the sky. Do you see God? You cannot see God, but He sees you right now. He really likes it when you learn about Him. He gets excited when He sees you doing what is right. He is always looking for you to be like Him.

Dear Jesus, help me know You are looking at me right now. I know You are excited when I learn about you.

God is looking at you now.

God Takes Care of You

> The Lord . . . will give you strength and protect you.
>
> 2 Thessalonians 3:3

Have you ever gotten scared at night? If you called for your mom and dad, they probably came in and made you feel better. Did you know that when you are afraid you can pray to God and He will be with you? When it is dark in your room at night, God will take care of you. When someone hurts you, God will take care of you. God always takes care of you.

Dear Lord, I know You are looking at me right now. Please take care of me tonight.

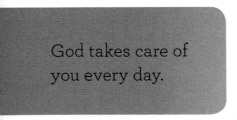

God takes care of you every day.

Dr. Ronnie Floyd, Cross Church, Northwest Arkansas

God Helps You!

So our hope is in the Lord. He is our help, our shield to protect us.

Psalm 33:20

D o you ever help your mom or dad? They like it when you help them pull weeds in the garden or clean up your toys. Just like you help them, God helps you. God helps you when you are having a hard day. God makes you feel better when you are hurt. When someone makes fun of you, God will help you. He is always with you.

Dear Jesus, thank You for helping me. Thank You for being there for me. Show me how to help others like You help me.

Remember, God is always there to help you.

God Protects You!

Protect me as a bird protects its
young under its wings.

Psalm 61:4

When a mother bird has little baby birds, she takes care of them. The mother bird does not let anyone or anything hurt the baby birds. God does the same for you. When God protects you, He keeps you safe. He takes care of you in every way. God protects you every day in ways that you do not even know. God is protecting you all the time.

Dear God, thank You for protecting me. You protect me when I am asleep and when I am awake. Thank You for loving me that much.

God watches over you.

Have Faith in God

[The Lord] is a shield to those who trust him.

Psalm 18:30

God is always protecting you. God is always helping you. God is always taking care of you. This is why you can have faith in God. Faith means that you are trusting in Jesus and Him only. People are not perfect and make mistakes. But God's Word is true. And God will always love you perfectly. You can put your trust in Jesus.

Dear God, I have faith in You. I know You love me. I know You are with me every day. I trust only in You.

Have faith in God every day!

God Is Good

The Lord is good and right.

Psalm 25:8

The Bible says that God is perfect and everything He does is good. God has a beautiful plan for your life. He wants you to spend time with Him and love Him. He will always do what is right for you. You can trust Him because He always knows what is best for you.

Jesus, You are perfect! I trust you because everything You do is good.

God is always good.

April Mack, Grace Fellowship Church, Warren, OH

Play Fair

Learn to do good. Be fair to other
people.

Isaiah 1:17

Have you ever been around someone who did
not play fair? Have you ever been the one
who didn't follow the rules? Imagine playing a
game with Jesus. He would always play fair. Jesus
would always share. Jesus would always be kind.
You should treat others like Jesus would treat them.
How do you want others to treat you? You should
always treat your family and friends like you want
to be treated.

Jesus, help me play fair and
treat people the way You
would treat them.

God is always fair.

Jesus Forgives

It is good to be kind and generous.
Psalm 112:5

Have you ever been mad at your friends? Maybe they were mean to you or did something wrong that hurt you. Some people were mean to Jesus, but Jesus prayed for them. When He was on the cross, He asked God to forgive the people who were hurting Him. Jesus was forgiving even to those who were hurting Him.

Jesus is also generous. Not only does He forgive you, but He blesses you with many wonderful things. Can you name some gifts that He has given you? His greatest gift to you is His forgiveness when you do something wrong.

Jesus, thank You for forgiving me and blessing my family.

Jesus is our gift.

God Loves Israel

God is truly good to Israel, to those who have pure hearts.

Psalm 73:1

Israel is a special place to God. God loves the people of Israel. He wants them all to know His Son, Jesus. Jesus wants to be a friend to the people of Israel. Jesus wants to be our friend too. When you ask Jesus to be your Savior, He forgives your sins and gives you a pure heart. Have you asked Jesus to be your friend and Savior?

Jesus, thank You for being my friend. I pray for Israel, that they would know you as their friend.

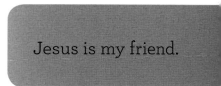

Jesus is my friend.

April Mack, Grace Fellowship Church, Warren, OH

Pleasing God

The Lord is pleased with a good person.

Proverbs 12:2

What are some good things you do? Do you obey your parents? Do you clean your room? God is pleased when you do good things. You should always want to please God. You please God when you do your best. You please God when you have good manners. You please God when you are kind to others. God has done so much for us, and we show Him that we love Him when we do good things for others.

Jesus, help me be good. I want to do good things for other people.

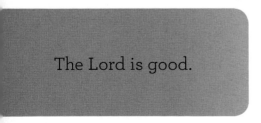

The Lord is good.

April Mack, Grace Fellowship Church, Warren, OH

God Blesses Me

Every good action and every perfect
gift is from God.

James 1:17

D o you like to receive gifts for your birthday
or Christmas? Do you know that God gives
you gifts too? He blesses you with the ability to do
special things, like playing music, singing, or being
good in sports. What are the gifts He has given
you? The best gift He gives us is Jesus. Jesus is the
gift that helps us to do our best with all of our other
gifts.

Jesus, thank You for being a gift
to me.

I am blessed.

Overflowing Blessings

And God can give you more blessings than you need. Then you will always have plenty of everything.

2 Corinthians 9:8

Have you ever gone to get ice cream and your parents got you an extra scoop? Chocolate and vanilla! Yum! You did not need both scoops, but they sure did taste good. Your parents like to surprise you with treats. God is your heavenly Father, and He enjoys blessing you too! He gives you everything you need and more. His blessings overflow in your life if you look for them.

Jesus, thank You for giving me more than I need.

God gives me overflowing blessings.

Play Ball

It is God who makes us able to do
all that we do.

2 Corinthians 3:5

D o you remember the first time you threw
a ball to your mom or dad? At first, you
probably had a hard time throwing, but you got
better with practice. Did you know it is God who
gives you the ability to do things like throwing and
catching a ball? God made you, and He makes you
able to run, draw pictures, and read books. God
is with you every day. He makes you able to do
everything you do.

Jesus, thank You for making me. You help me do all the
things I do.

God helps me do
everything.

Prize Picture

But in all these things we have full victory through God who showed his love for us.

Romans 8:37

D o you like painting pictures? It is fun to experiment with paint. You can use your imagination and use lots of different colors. Have you ever gotten a prize or a ribbon for one of your drawings? It feels so good to get a prize for something you did. God shows His love to us by giving us the best prize ever. He gave us Jesus. And we did not have to do anything to earn that prize! Jesus died on the cross to take away our sins because He loves us. We have victory in Jesus.

Jesus, thank You for loving me. You gave me victory over my sins by dying on the cross for me.

Jesus loves me!

Michele Rummage, Bell Shoals Baptist Church, Brandon, FL

Daily Blessings

Praise be to the God and Father of
our Lord Jesus Christ. In Christ,
God has given us every spiritual
blessing in heaven.

Ephesians 1:3

It is great fun to go to the park and play with
your friends. You can swing on the swings
together. You can pretend to be explorers looking
for buried treasure. You can play in the sand and
build strange creations. It is a blessing to hang
out with your friends and just be together. One of
the greatest blessings is being friends with Jesus.
Your friend Jesus blesses you with
everything you have.

Jesus, thank You for being my
friend and blessing me. I praise
You for loving me.

Jesus blesses me
every day.

Victory in Jesus

But we thank God! He gives us the victory through our Lord Jesus Christ.

1 Corinthians 15:57

Many schools have a Field Day where kids get to run races, shoot basketballs, jump ropes, and have fun. One of the best parts of the day is a ceremony when boys and girls receive prizes for competing. God's greatest prize is the one that Jesus won when He died on the cross. Jesus died to take away our sins. Sins are bad things that do not please God. When we ask Jesus, God will give us His prize of forgiveness.

God, thank You for sending Your Son, Jesus, to take away my sins.

Jesus died for me!

Jesus the Superhero

So what should we say about this?
If God is with us, then no one can
defeat us.

Romans 8:31

D o you like to dress up as a superhero or a
princess? You can pretend you are Spider-
man, Iron Man, or Captain America. You can be
Cinderella, Snow White, or Jasmine. It is fun to
pretend that your teddy bear has been captured
and you have to rescue him. It is fun to play the
hero. The Bible tells us that Jesus is our hero. He is
with us all the time. When Jesus is with us, no one
can defeat us.

Jesus, thank You for always being with me. You are my
hero.

God is with me.

Michele Rummage, Bell Shoals Baptist Church, Brandon, FL   103

Jesus Forgives and Forgets

> "I, I am the One who forgives all your sins. . . . I will not remember your sins."
>
> Isaiah 43:25

The Israelites were God's people, but they were not doing the things God asked them to do. They were not obeying God and so their lives were difficult. But God loved them so much that He forgave them. He said He would forget what they had done wrong and never think of it again. He loves you that much too! God, who can do everything, chooses not to remember the wrong things we do when we tell Him we are sorry.

Thank You, God, for forgiving me when I do something wrong. Thank You for not remembering the bad things I do. Thank You for loving me that much!

God does not remember the wrong things I have done.

Dr. Mary Dighton, Lenexa Baptist Church, Lenexa, KS

Jesus Always Hears and Helps

Lord, hear my voice. Listen to my prayer for help.

Psalm 130:2

No one is perfect. No one does the right thing all the time. It is hard to always be good, and sometimes we feel really bad about the way we act. God is listening to us even when we feel like He isn't. He wants to help us be more like Him. The Bible tells us that God always hears us when we pray. He will always help us when we ask Him to. We know that with His help we can do what is right.

God, thank You that I can believe what the Bible says. Thank You for listening to me when I pray and helping me when I ask.

Jesus always listens when we ask Him for help.

Be Like Jesus

If someone does wrong to you, then forgive him. Forgive each other because the Lord forgave you.

Colossians 3:13

When we learn about Jesus from the Bible, we know how to live our lives. He is our example. He tells us and shows us what to do. When people were not nice to Him, He forgave them just like He forgives you when you do not obey Him. We always want Jesus to forgive us, but sometimes we are mad and do not feel like forgiving other people. Jesus is our example of what to do. We are like Jesus when we forgive people who are not nice to us.

Jesus, thank You for always forgiving me. Help me be more like You so I will always forgive others.

Jesus shows me how to forgive.

Happy Prayers

"When you are praying, and you remember that you are angry with another person about something, then forgive him."

Mark 11:25

J esus always does what is right. When we are mad at people and we do not forgive them, we are not obeying Jesus. We feel unhappy when we are mad and when we do not obey. Jesus wants the best for us, and He knows that we will feel good when we obey Him. If you do what Jesus asks you to do, you will be happy.

Jesus, thank You for wanting the best for me. Thank You for teaching me that I will be happy when I obey You. Thank You for listening to my prayers.

God says to forgive others before we pray.

Jesus Already Knows

> But if we confess our sins, he will forgive our sins.
>
> 1 John 1:9

Jesus knows everything. You cannot hide anything from Him. When you do something wrong, tell Him about it. Ask Him to forgive you and help you not to do it again. He loves you and wants to help you be more like Him. Tell Jesus you are sorry about the wrong things you have done and ask Him to forgive you.

Jesus, please forgive me when I do something wrong. Help me obey Your Word. Thank You for always loving me.

Jesus forgives me when I ask Him to.

Dr. Mary Dighton, Lenexa Baptist Church, Lenexa, KS

Jesus Sets Us Free

In Christ we are set free . . . so we have forgiveness.

Ephesians 1:7

Jesus is perfect. He never displeased God or did anything wrong to deserve being punished. Sometimes we make God sad because we do not obey Him. We deserve to be punished. But the Bible tells us that when we know Jesus, we do not have to be afraid of being punished by God. Because Jesus loves us so much, He took our punishment for us. We should always listen to Jesus and obey Him because He loves us so much!

Thank You, Jesus, for taking the punishment for the things I have done wrong. Help me listen and obey my parents as they teach me what the Bible says.

Jesus was punished for me, so I don't have to be afraid.

Are You on God's Team?

Whoever says that God lives in him must live as Jesus lived.

1 John 2:6

Do you have a favorite sports team? When we are really big fans of a team, we wear the uniform of our favorite players. When you decide you want to be on God's team, you become God's child—just like Jesus. Jesus is the greatest player on God's team, and He is the player we want to be like!

God, thank You for letting me be on Your team. I love You, Jesus. Thank You for loving me first.

My favorite team is God's team!

Obey or Disobey?

That is what you were called to do.
[Christ] gave you an example to follow.
So you should do as he did.

1 Peter 2:21

D o you have a dog? If you don't, maybe you
know someone who does. Some dogs listen
really well, but some are still puppies who don't
obey their owners yet. When dogs get older, they
have fun learning more and more things. When
they do the right thing for their owner, it makes
them so happy! That's how we are with God. Every
time we obey Him, it makes us happy. And God is
happy when we obey too.

God, help me obey You at all times. I love You, Jesus.
Thank You for loving me first.

Obeying God makes
Him happy.

Becoming a Lion

You are God's children whom he loves. So try to be like God.

Ephesians 5:1

L ions are just tiny cubs when they're born. But their dads are huge, with powerful bodies and furry manes. Grown-up lions are the kings of the jungle, and they love their babies. Lion cubs want to be big and strong just like the kings of the jungle. When somebody loves you as much as God does, you want to be just like Him! Even when you make mistakes, no matter how old you are, God still loves you and wants you to be like Him.

God, You are a great King. I love You, Jesus. Thank You for loving me first.

God is the King of everything. I want to be more like Him.

Caz McCaslin, Upward Sports, Spartanburg, SC

Using What We Have

In your lives you must think and act like Christ Jesus.

Philippians 2:5

One time Jesus was teaching five thousand people, and they all got hungry! Jesus' disciples were worried because there wasn't enough food for everyone. One little boy had a little bit of fish and bread. He shared all that he had, even though it wasn't much. Jesus prayed over the food, and God provided enough for everyone to eat! When we share, it helps others just like the little boy did.

God, help me use what I have to help others. I love You, Jesus. Thank You for loving me first.

Jesus can use what I have, even if it's not much.

How Can I Serve?

"I, your Lord and Teacher, have
washed your feet. So you also should
wash each other's feet."

John 13:14

Have you ever gone to a restaurant and had a
waiter bring your food to you? Wasn't that
nice? You didn't have to do anything. But Jesus
said that it is more fun for us to do things for other
people than for them to do things for us. Why don't
you try it? The next time your family is together for
a meal, bring someone their food, just like a waiter,
and see how fun it is!

God, help me want to help
others like You did. I love
You, Jesus. Thank You for
loving me first.

It is more fun to serve
than to be served.

The Greatest Gift Ever

This is how we know what real love is: Jesus gave his life for us.

1 John 3:16

T hink about all the cool things you got for Christmas last year. Which one of those was your absolute favorite present? What if you took that present and gave it to somebody who wasn't able to get any presents for Christmas? That would be really, really hard. But that's what God did when He sent His Son, Jesus, to us to take away all our sins. God gave us His greatest gift.

God, thank You for the gift of Your Son. I love You, Jesus. Thank You for loving me first.

The greatest gift of all is God's Son, Jesus.

What Do I Really Need?

My God will use his wonderful riches in Christ Jesus to give you everything you need.

Philippians 4:19

Do you say, "I want" a lot? You want a new toy or game, you want to play with a friend, and you want to stay up past your bedtime. Every day there are things that we want, and we might get upset when we do not get them. Just because you want something does not mean you need it or that it is good for you. God knows exactly what you need. If you believe in Jesus and obey what He tells you, you will have everything you need.

Jesus, thank You for giving me everything I need and sometimes things I want. Thank You for loving my family, my friends, and me.

God gives us everything we need.

Amy Dixon, Liberty Baptist Church, Dublin, GA

Christ Makes Me Strong

I can do all things through Christ because he gives me strength.
Philippians 4:13

Have you ever felt weak, scared, or not strong enough to do something? The Bible reminds us that sometimes we are not strong enough, brave enough, or big enough to do things on our own. Jesus wants us to ask Him for help. You may be having trouble with homework, getting along with your brother or sister, starting a new school, or learning a new sport. Whatever you need help with, Jesus reminds us that He is with us and He will give us His strength to do all things.

Jesus, thank You that I can come to You anytime I feel weak, scared, or worried, and You will strengthen me.

Jesus loves me so much.
He makes me stronger.

Living with God

Good people will inherit the land.
They will live in it forever.

Psalm 37:29

Who are the good people this verse talks about? They are the ones who love and obey God's Word. The land this verse is talking about is heaven. The Bible tells us that if you want to live with God forever in heaven, then you must ask Him to forgive your sins and love Him. Loving and obeying God every day of your life is why God created you! He loves you and wants to live with you forever!

Jesus, thank You for loving me so much that You died for me so I can live with You forever!

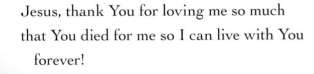

God wants me to live with Him forever!

Talking with God

"So I tell you to ask for things in prayer."

Mark 11:24

G od gave us prayer so that we can talk to Him every day—just like we do with our parents, grandparents, teachers, and friends. We can pray about anything when we talk to God. We can ask God to help us have a good day at school, or we can pray for someone who is sick. When we are afraid, we can ask God to keep us safe. If we are sad or upset, we can ask God to comfort us. The most important prayer we can pray is for other boys and girls all over the world to ask Jesus to come into their hearts.

Jesus, thank You for giving us prayer so that we can talk to You about everything. Thank You for loving us.

God cares about everything we do.

Amy Dixon, Liberty Baptist Church, Dublin, GA

119

Share the Good News!

God gave us the work of bringing everyone into peace with him.

2 Corinthians 5:18

What is the greatest news you have ever heard? Did you want to keep the news to yourself? Have you ever received a gift and were so excited that you wanted to tell others about it? God gave us the gift of His love. He wants us to tell others who He is and how much He loves everyone. God gave us the greatest gift when He gave us Jesus. To be a good friend, we must share who God is. Pray that others will ask Jesus to forgive them of their sins so that they can live with Him forever.

Thank You, God, for sending Your Son, Jesus, to save me. Help me tell others about You so they can have forgiveness too!

We must tell others how much God loves them.

Amy Dixon, Liberty Baptist Church, Dublin, GA

He Chose Us First!

[God] chose us before the world was made.

Ephesians 1:4

D id you know that God knew you before you were even born? He knew your name and what you would like and not like. He knew everything about you and knows everything about you today. Pretty cool, huh? Did you know that God chose to love you before the world was made? He chose to love you before the moon, stars, and sun were created. God chose to love you a long time ago, and He loves you today. He wants you to choose to love Him and live your life every day with Him.

Thank You, Jesus, for loving me, dying on the cross for me, and forgiving me for all of my sins. I am thankful You chose me.

Jesus chose me.

God Makes Me Safe

The Lord God is like our sun and shield. The Lord gives us kindness and glory.

Psalm 84:11

God wants you to know that He is on your side. You do not need to be afraid because Jesus is with you and protects you. God is strong. Have you ever seen a picture of a knight holding a shield? It is big and strong and keeps the knight safe. God promises that He is your shield. When you feel afraid, remember that Jesus is with you and will protect you.

Dear God, thank You for keeping me safe. Help me remember how big You are.

I will not be afraid because God protects me and is with me.

God Makes Me Special

The Spirit that God made to live in us wants us for himself alone.

James 4:5

We know that God lives in heaven, but He also has a place to live on earth. He does not live in the church building. He lives in the people who believe in Him. When God lives in you, He makes you very special. God is happy to be so close to you. He is your God and your best friend. He wants to be the most important thing in your life.

Dear God, thank You for making me. I enjoy being with You.

Do not forget that God made you special.

Dr. Clayton Cloer, First Baptist Church of Central Florida, Orlando, FL

123

God Will Never Let You Down

The Lord's love never ends. His
mercies never stop.

Lamentations 3:22

God created the world in six days. Then, on the
seventh day, God stopped. God had sixty-six
books written in the Bible, and then He stopped.
God can stop doing some things. But God can
never stop loving His children, and He will never
stop forgiving them. God will never, ever let you
down. His love cannot run out. God's love lasts
forever.

Dear God, thank You for always giving me mercy and
love. I love You and thank You. Help me always trust You,
even when life is hard.

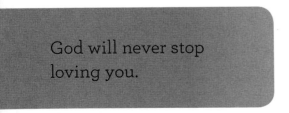

God will never stop
loving you.

Dr. Clayton Cloer, First Baptist Church of Central Florida,
Orlando, FL

Jesus Brings the Most Fun in Life

"I came to give life—life in all its fullness."

John 10:10

J esus came to the earth to show people how to have the best life. He had children around Him so much because He loved them. He took care of people who were hurting. He fed people who came to hear Him speak. When a storm came up, He protected His friends. He went to other people's houses, and they had a lot of fun together. Jesus made sad people happy. Jesus brings the best out of life.

Dear God, I want all the good things that You want to give me. Thank You for wanting to give me such a great life.

God has everything. He wants us to enjoy what He has.

Give Thanks and Have a Good Attitude

So let us be thankful because we have a kingdom that cannot be shaken.

Hebrews 12:28

Sometimes we have a bad attitude and complain. We may complain about our food, the weather, or our clothes. We should not complain because God is so good to us. We should be thankful for all that we have. It is ugly to have a bad attitude. It hurts God when we complain. Jesus died for us on the cross. We get to be with God forever! We should not complain because God loves us!

Dear God, help me remember all You have done for me. Thank You for everything. I love You.

Thank God for all He has given you.

You Can Trust Jesus

You believe in God through Christ.
God raised Christ from death and
gave him glory. So your faith and
your hope are in God.

1 Peter 1:21

When your mom tells you something, do you believe her? Sure you do. It hurts your mom's heart if you do not trust her. She loves you and only wants the best for you. God loves you, and it hurts God when you do not trust Jesus. Jesus died for our sins. He took our punishment at the cross. If we trust Him, then we can live with Him in heaven forever.

Dear God, thank You that You always tell the truth. I do not want to hurt Your heart. Help me remember that I can always trust You.

I trust God by believing His Word.

Dr. Clayton Cloer, First Baptist Church of Central Florida, Orlando, FL

A Special Teacher

"But when the Spirit of truth comes he will lead you into all truth."

John 16:13

Kali wanted to learn to play the piano. But Kali learned quickly that playing the piano was hard. Her mom introduced her to Mrs. Jan. She knew a lot about the piano, and she was a very good teacher. By listening to her teacher, Kali learned to play the piano well.

When Jesus went back to heaven, He gave us a special teacher to help us learn more about God. Our special teacher is the Holy Spirit. In today's verse, He is called the Spirit of truth. The Holy Spirit will help us understand the Bible and know what to do to please God.

Jesus, thank You for sending the Holy Spirit to be my guide and my special teacher. Help me learn what pleases You.

The Holy Spirit is our teacher.

When I Am Worried

He will guide us into the path that goes toward peace.

Luke 1:79

Kennedy's mom was sick. Her mom took some medicine and was resting. Her dad said that God was going to help her mom feel better tomorrow. Kennedy loved her mom. She was worried and a little bit afraid.

Jesus does not want us to worry. He is strong enough to take care of us. He wants us to trust Him when things bother us. Jesus will help us. He can take away our worry and give us peace.

Jesus, when I am afraid, please help me trust You and not worry.

Jesus is strong enough to take care of my problems.

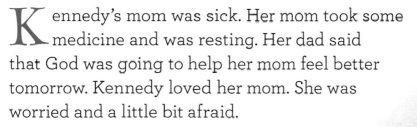

When I Am Afraid

The Lord says, "I will make you wise. I will show you where to go. I will guide you and watch over you."

Psalm 32:8

Max was afraid. There was a storm outside with lightning and thunder. Suddenly the lights went out and it was totally dark. Max could not see his toys or even where to walk. Then he heard his dad say, "Max, stay where you are. I am coming." His dad brought him a flashlight, and then Max could see where to go.

The Bible says that God will guide us. When we do not know what to do, God will show us the right choice. God is always watching over us to protect us.

Jesus, thank You for showing me what I should do and where I should go.

Jesus will always watch over me.

When Things Change

This God is our God forever and
ever. He will guide us from now on.
                    Psalm 48:14

S arah and Addison had been friends for a
long time. They talked, played, and laughed
together. But now Addison was moving far away to
a new town. Sarah was sad and a little angry that
Addison had to move. Everything was just right.
Sarah did not want her to go away.

When things change, sometimes it is hard.
Sometimes we do not like change. But God
promises to be our God forever and ever. He will
never change. He will always be our friend.

Jesus, thank You for my friends. But I thank You most
for being my friend forever.

Jesus never changes.

When I Disobey

God has been very kind to you, and
he has been patient with you.

Romans 2:4

Trent knew he was in trouble. His mom asked him to put all his toys away. But Trent disobeyed. He kept on playing and even got out more toys. Now his mom was coming to his room and Trent thought he was in big trouble. But his mom said she was giving him another chance to obey and put his toys away. Trent's mom was being patient with him.

The Bible tells us that God is very kind. Even when we disobey, He loves us and is patient with us. He wants us to obey our parents and Him the first time, but He will never stop loving us, no matter what we do.

Jesus, thank You for being patient with me when I disobey You. Thank You for forgiving me. Help me obey You the first time.

Jesus is kind even when we disobey.

Bob McCartney, First Baptist Church, Wichita Falls, TX

Jesus Takes Care of Me

"I am the good shepherd. The good shepherd gives his life for the sheep."
John 10:11

A shepherd takes care of sheep. The shepherd leads sheep to water and good food. He also protects the sheep from animals that would harm them. If a sheep gets sick, the shepherd helps it get better.

Jesus said that He is our Good Shepherd. As our Good Shepherd, we can trust Jesus to take good care of us. He will give us what we need. He will protect us. He will help us when we are sick. Jesus cares about us.

Jesus, thank You for being my Good Shepherd. Thank You for caring for me. Thank You for giving me what I need each day.

Jesus takes care of us.

Who Will Save Me?

The Lord is my light and the one who saves me. I fear no one. The Lord protects my life. I am afraid of no one.

Psalm 27:1

Have you ever heard a strange or loud noise that scared you? Are you sometimes afraid of the dark? God wants you to know that He is stronger than anything that might frighten you. He is always with you. God will protect you. God is like a light in the darkness, and you can always trust Him to show you the way!

Thank You, God, for keeping me safe. I know You are here to take care of me.

The Lord keeps me safe!

God Is Powerful

The Lord is powerful. He gives
power and victory to his chosen one.
Psalm 28:8

D avid heard that a giant named Goliath was saying bad things about God. David loved God very much, so he grabbed a slingshot and a rock to stand up to Goliath. David knew that he did not have to be afraid of his enemies because the Lord was with him. David won the battle and defeated the giant. Hooray! God loves us and takes care of us. You can trust Him to keep you safe.

Thank You, Lord, for protecting me. Because You are with me, I will not be afraid.

The Lord gives me power
and courage when I need it.

Sweet Peace

The Lord gives strength to his
people. The Lord blesses his people
with peace.

Psalm 29:11

Jesus and His disciples were on a boat when a
storm blew in. The wind blew so hard that it
rocked the boat. The disciples thought they might
crash! The disciples asked Jesus for help. Guess
what? Jesus told the rain and the wind, "Hush! Be
still!" The water got calm, and the rain and wind
stopped. Everything was peaceful again. Jesus is
so strong even the wind and rain listen to Him!

Thank You, Jesus, for being strong. When I feel scared, I
know You will give me peace.

Jesus gives me peace
when things get rough.

Michelle Bowen, Heritage Church, Moultrie, GA

Where Should I Go?

The Lord saves good people. He is
their strong city in times of trouble.
Psalm 37:39

I magine a castle with huge walls made of stone.
How strong do you think those walls are?
Castles used to be built to protect people. Inside
a castle, people were safe from anyone who might
want to hurt them. God tells us that we can run to
Him anytime we are scared or in trouble, and He
will protect us—just like the walls of a great big
castle!

Thank You, God, that You are a safe place
for me when I am afraid. Thank You for
saving me from trouble.

The Lord is my
protector.

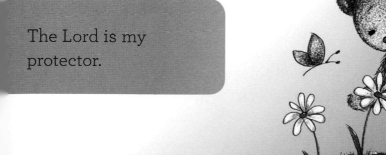

God Answers Prayers

On the day I called to you, you answered me. You made me strong and brave.

Psalm 138:3

Once there was a man named Daniel who loved God very much. But one day, some bad people who did not believe in God took Daniel and threw him into a dangerous pit full of lions. Yikes! Daniel prayed, and God sent an angel to keep him safe. The lions did not hurt Daniel one bit. It was a miracle! Daniel was not afraid because he knew God would protect him.

Thank You, God, that You listen when I talk to You. Thank You for making me strong and brave.

God listens to me when I talk to Him.

God Is So Strong!

"My grace is enough for you. When you are weak, then my power is made perfect in you."

2 Corinthians 12:9

Have you ever watched a little baby? They are so cute and snuggly, but they need lots of attention. Babies are weak, so God gives them a loving family to help take care of them. Do you ever feel weak? Me too! Sometimes we all need help. God loves us so much that He promises to take care of us, just like a parent taking care of a precious baby.

Thank You, God, for loving me and taking care of me. Your love and power are perfect for me!

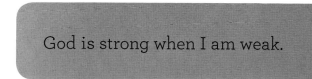

God is strong when I am weak.

A Great Reward

You must hold on, so you can do what God wants and receive what he has promised.

Hebrews 10:36

God has planned a great reward for His children. A reward is like a present or a prize. He has promised that if we love Him, one day we will get to be with Him forever. When that happens, there will be no more sickness, no more crying, and no more pain! Wow!

Sometimes we go through sad things on earth. It is part of life here. But God promises that one day we will not be sad anymore! We get to live in heaven with God forever!

God, thank You that one day I will be with You forever.

I get to live in heaven with Jesus forever!

Dr. Grant Ethridge, Liberty Baptist Church, Hampton, VA / Suffolk, VA

Big Family

But Christ is faithful as a Son who is the head of God's family.

Hebrews 3:6

Jesus is God's Son. We become part of God's family by loving Jesus. God loves you so much. He wants to call you His own son or daughter. Everyone who loves Jesus is part of God's family too. Isn't it great that we can be a part of the family of God!

God, thank You that I can be part of Your family. Help me love You and love others.

I am part of God's family.

Doing What Is Right

You know that Christ is righteous.
So you know that all who do what is
right are God's children.

1 John 2:29

Jesus always did the right thing. Even when His friends did something bad, He did what God wanted Him to do. Because of His actions, people knew that He was God's Son. God was very proud of Him. God wants us to do the right thing too. Even when we think no one is watching, God sees. When He sees us doing right, it makes Him smile. It also lets others know that we are His children.

Jesus, help me do right even when it is hard. I want to make You happy, and I want others to know that I am Your child.

God smiles when I do the right thing.

You Are Heard

We can come to God with no doubts. This means that when we ask God for things (and those things agree with what God wants for us), then God cares about what we say.

1 John 5:14

D o you ever feel like you have something to say, but the person you are trying to talk to is not listening? It is not fun to be ignored. We all like to be heard. The Bible tells us that we can be sure God hears us when we pray. No matter how big or little our problem, God cares about it. He wants to hear from you! What a great promise to know that when we pray, God hears!

God, thank You that You hear me when I pray. I am glad I can know that You care about what I have to say.

God hears me when I pray.

Dr. Grant Ethridge, Liberty Baptist Church,
Hampton, VA / Suffolk, VA

Do Not Be Afraid

The Lord will keep you safe. He will keep you from being trapped.

Proverbs 3:26

God promises to keep us safe. Sometimes we are scared because of a real danger, and sometimes we are scared because of something we made up. Everyone feels scared at times. But God promises that when we are afraid, He will be with us.

No matter what you fear, Jesus is bigger and stronger than anything that makes you scared. He will never leave you alone. God is always there. You do not have to be afraid because He is with you!

Jesus, thank You for keeping me safe. I do not have to be afraid because You are always with me.

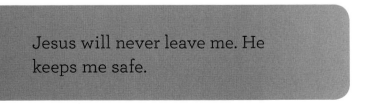

Jesus will never leave me. He keeps me safe.

Dr. Grant Ethridge, Liberty Baptist Church, Hampton, VA / Suffolk, VA

Promise Keeper

We can trust God to do what he promised.

Hebrews 10:23

A promise is doing what you say. If you make a promise, you should not break it. Sometimes, though, people break promises, even when they do not mean to. God makes us promises throughout the Bible. He promises to help us, to be with us, to comfort us, to provide for us, and so much more. Even though people do not always keep their promises, God will. The Bible is God's Word, and it is always true. We can be sure that if God said something, He will do it!

God, thank You that You always keep Your promises. Even if I cannot see how, You will do what You say.

Jesus keeps His promises.

When You Are Feeling Sick

Peter said to him, "Aeneas, Jesus Christ heals you. Stand up and make your bed!"

Acts 9:34

We all get sick. That is why we sometimes need to go to the doctor, even though we do not like to. Jesus knows when we get sick. He knows when we feel bad. He is always watching over us. When He was on earth, He healed many sick people, and in the Bible we read that even after He went back to heaven, He still healed people. He still does today!

Jesus, thank You for always watching over me and healing me when I get sick.

Jesus is the greatest doctor of all.

I Can Ask God to Heal Others

Pray for each other. Do this so that God can heal you. When a good man prays, great things happen.

James 5:16

Whenever you talk to God, He is always listening. He loves it when we talk to Him and especially when we talk to Him about others who are sick. Do you have a friend or someone in your family who is sick? God wants you to ask Him to help them feel better and get well. Do you know of someone you could pray for right now?

Dear God, I pray for this sick person right now. Please heal them and make them well. I know You can heal any sickness, and I thank You for hearing my prayer.

God hears and God heals.

Dr. James Merritt, Cross Pointe Church, Duluth, GA

A Sunny Promise for You

"For you who honor me, goodness will shine on you like the sun. There will be healing in its rays."

Malachi 4:2

D o you love going out on a sunny day to play? Does the warm sun feel good on your face? God says when we love Him and obey Him, we will feel His goodness and love in our hearts. It will feel like the sun shining on our bodies. When we live for God, it makes us feel good all over! So the next time you see the sun, thank God for how good He is!

God, help me remember how good You are every time I see the sun. I love You, God!

The sunshine tells me every day that God loves me!

I Can Obey God's Rules

"You must obey all [God's] laws and keep his rules. . . . I am the Lord. I am the Lord who heals you."

Exodus 15:26

God gives us rules to help us be happy and healthy. God tells us that if we obey His rules, we will not get into trouble. We will feel better and even sleep better. God knows what will hurt us or make us sad. He wants us to be happy and safe. So whenever God tells you to do something, always remember God wants what is best for you.

Father, help me today to obey You in every way!

It is always best to obey God.

When You Are Feeling Sad

He heals the brokenhearted. He bandages their wounds.

Psalm 147:3

There are two ways we can hurt. We can hurt on the outside and on the inside. When we get a cut on our finger, we can get a Band-Aid. But what about when we are sad on the inside? God can put His Band-Aid of love on our hearts and help us feel better. He does this by reminding us He will always take care of us. Do you hurt on the inside? Tell God about it—He will help you.

Dear God, thank You for helping me when I hurt on the inside or the outside.

God's love always makes my hurts better.

Who Can Heal Me?

Jesus healed all the sick.
Matthew 8:16

Wouldn't it be great to be a doctor who could heal any sickness? Even the best doctor in the world cannot do that because some people are too sick for any doctor to heal. But Jesus can heal any sickness because Jesus is God! Jesus always heals sick people. Sometimes He heals them on earth for a little while. Sometimes He heals them in heaven forever. But Jesus always heals!

Lord Jesus, I am so glad that You are my doctor forever! One day in heaven no one will be sick anymore! Thank You for loving me. I love You too!

Jesus can heal anybody anytime.

Dr. James Merritt, Cross Pointe Church, Duluth, GA

Just Being with You!

You will teach me God's way to live.
Being with you will fill me with joy.
Psalm 16:11

Who is your favorite person to spend time with? When you are with this special person, you probably do not even think about the time until your parents say, "It's time to go." You don't want to leave because you are having such a great time! Did you know the Lord loves it when you spend time with Him? When you pray, read the Bible, or go to church, you are spending time with Jesus. You can talk to Him all the time, no matter where you are or what you are doing. This makes Him very happy, and it will make you happy too!

Lord, I'm glad You want to spend time with me. Help me not let anything keep me from spending time with You.

There's nothing better than being with Jesus.

Pastor Jeff Crook, Blackshear Place Baptist Church, Flowery Branch, GA

The Best Gift!

"Ask and you will receive. And your joy will be the fullest joy."

John 16:24

Billy asked his dad for a bike for his birthday. The day came, and Billy was so excited—he got a bike! He ran and hugged his dad, saying, "I love the bike, but the greatest gift is a dad like you!" Billy loved the gift, but he loved the giver more. The Bible teaches us to ask when we need something, and God will bless us. But the joy is not the gifts. It is having God as our Father. He never leaves us and always loves us.

God, I love the things You give me. I want You to know I love You more!

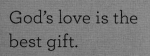

God's love is the best gift.

Never Without Hope

I pray that the God who gives hope
will fill you with much joy and peace
while you trust in him.

Romans 15:13

Have you ever lost something important to you? You searched for it and could not find it. Maybe you felt sad because you thought you would never find it again. Sometimes people feel very sad and lonely when they think they have lost everything. This is why everyone needs Jesus. He gives us hope. If we have Jesus, we can never lose Him. This means we are never without hope.

Jesus, You are my hope, and You never disappoint me. I can trust You at all times and for all things.

My hope is in Jesus.

Listen to God's Word

You accepted the teaching with the
joy that comes from the Holy Spirit.
1 Thessalonians 1:6

Do you listen in church when your pastor is talking about the Bible? Are your ears open in Sunday school when the lesson is taught? You are respecting God when you listen to His Word. It makes Jesus sad when we play with our iPods or whisper to our friends instead of listening. God talks to us when the Bible is taught. How rude to not listen to God! It is also foolish because we may miss something very important He wants us to hear.

God, help me be a good listener to Your Word and obey with a joyful heart. Your Word teaches me and shows me Your love.

God talks to our heart
through His Word.

Pastor Jeff Crook, Blackshear Place Baptist Church,
Flowery Branch, GA

No Good-byes

"I will see you again and you will be happy. And no one will take away your joy."

John 16:22

Good-byes are very hard. Jesus told His disciples that He was going to go back to heaven. Can you imagine how sad they were? The disciples loved spending time with Jesus and did not want Him to leave. Jesus reminded them that He wasn't really saying good-bye, but "see you later." They did not have to be sad because they were going to be with Him in heaven one day. When we love Jesus, we get to be with Him forever too! Smile right now and thank Jesus that there are really no good-byes for those who love Him.

Jesus, You always keep Your promises, and that puts a smile on my face and in my heart. I love and trust You.

I am not worried because I have Jesus.

Pastor Jeff Crook, Blackshear Place Baptist Church, Flowery Branch, GA

Our Best Friend

"I have told you these things so that you can have the same joy I have. I want your joy to be the fullest joy."
John 15:11

A true friend wants the best for you, not the worst. A friend would never want you to get hurt. Remember, the devil is not our friend. The Bible says he tries to make us sad and get us to do the wrong thing. Jesus is our friend. He gives us life, peace, and joy, and most of all, Himself! He said, "I am joyful, and I want you to be joyful too!" What an awesome friend Jesus is, and He wants to be your best friend!

Jesus, You are such a good friend. I want You to be my best friend. Thank You for giving me Your joy!

Jesus gives us His joy.

Always Do What Is Right

Try to live in the right way, serve God,
have faith, love, patience, and gentleness.
1 Timothy 6:11

Is it hard for you to do the right thing? Is it hard for you to listen to your parents? Is it hard for you to be nice to your brothers and sisters? Is it hard for you to be kind to other people? God wants us to be patient and kind toward others even when it is hard. He tells us in the Bible to have faith in Him and to love others. When we are kind, people can see the love of Jesus through our lives.

Jesus, thank You for giving me faith, love, patience, and gentleness. Even though it is sometimes hard to do the right thing, help me always treat others like You want me to treat them.

Jesus helps me show His love to others.

When It Is Hard to Wait

"They obey God's teaching and patiently produce good fruit."
Luke 8:15

Have you ever planted a seed and watched it grow? Sometimes it seems like it takes forever before a tiny seed becomes a plant. God wants us to obey Him and grow as a Christian, just like a tiny seed grows into a strong plant. It takes time, and we need to be patient.

Reading the Bible helps us know God. Knowing God helps us grow into the person God wants us to be. When we read the Bible, our faith, love, patience, and gentleness grow.

Jesus, thank You for giving me the Bible to teach me how to live for You. I know it takes time to grow into the person You want me to be. Help me wait on You.

Jesus gives me patience.

Looking Up to Others

Be like those who have faith and patience. They will receive what God has promised.

Hebrews 6:12

Who are the people you look up to? Maybe it is your mom and dad, your Sunday school teacher, your grandparents, or a favorite teacher at school. Do those people have faith and patience? God tells us in the Bible to look up to those who love Him. Make sure the people you choose to look up to love Jesus. People who love Jesus show faith, love, patience, and gentleness.

Jesus, thank You for giving me people in my life who love You. Help me love You like they do.

Jesus gives me godly people to look up to.

Macey Fossett, Fossett Evangelistic Ministries, Dalton, GA

Showing God's Love

Let your patience show itself
perfectly in what you do.

James 1:4

S ometimes bad things happen to us. God gives
us what we need to get through hard times.
Going through hard situations helps us grow into
the person God wants us to be. God wants us to
depend on Him. He promises to always be there
for us. When we get through the bad times, we can
give God the glory for taking care of us.

Jesus, thank You for being with me even when
times get hard. Help me depend on
You in every situation.

Jesus is there for
me even when
times get tough.

There Is Always Hope in Jesus

You, too, must be patient. Do not give up hope.

James 5:8

D o you have a hard time waiting? Do you say things like, "I want it right now"? Sometimes it is hard to wait for what we want. We need to trust that God will give us what we need. We should not give up hope. Even when we do not understand why we have to wait, we need to remember that God knows what is best for us. Trust God and believe that He will take care of you.

Jesus, thank You for always wanting what is best for me. Help me see Your plan for my life.

Jesus gives me hope.

Good Things Come from God

Patience and encouragement come from God.

> Romans 15:5

God knows that it is hard for us to be good. He tells us in the Bible that He gives us patience and encouragement so that we can make good choices. It is wise to be patient and pray about something before you do it, but it is not always easy to wait. God encourages us and gives us peace when we wait on Him to tell us what to do. God loves us so much. He wants to help us. All we have to do is ask Him.

Jesus, thank You for giving me patience and encouragement. Help me use the good things You give me to show Your love to others.

Jesus gives me what I need to be good.

Something New!

If anyone belongs to Christ, then he is made new. The old things have gone; everything is made new!

2 Corinthians 5:17

Toys often break. Arms come off of dolls. Tires come off of toy trucks. When a toy breaks, sometimes your mom or dad can fix it and make it like new again. God fixes things too. God can fix us. When we disobey God, we need to say, "I'm sorry. I love You, Jesus." Then He makes us new. He fixes us! You can talk to God right now and tell Him you are sorry and you love Him.

God, I am sorry. I love You, Jesus. Please make me new.

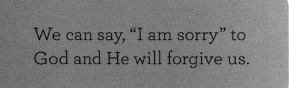

We can say, "I am sorry" to God and He will forgive us.

Dr. J. Kie Bowman, Hyde Park Baptist Church, Austin, TX

God's Gift to Jesus

All things were made through
Christ and for Christ.

Colossians 1:16

D o you like to play in the grass? Do you ever
play in the sand? Have you ever played in the
rain or in the snow? It is fun to go outside and play.
Did you know God wants us to have fun outside?
God made everything. He made the sun, the
clouds, and even the snow. Do you know why God
made everything? He made it all for Jesus! Jesus is
God's Son, and the world is God's present to Jesus!
And we get to enjoy it too!

Thank You, God, for making the
world for Your Son, Jesus!

God created everything
as a gift for Jesus.

God Wrote a Book!

God decided to give us life through the word of truth. He wanted us to be the most important of all the things he made.

James 1:18

Did you know the Bible is a book from God? The Bible tells us about Jesus and how to go to heaven. The Bible is God's book. God always tells the truth, and His book is true. That is why the Bible is sometimes called the Word of Truth. You should believe everything the Bible says. It is true!

God, thank You for giving me the Bible. I know it tells me the truth!

I can learn about Jesus from the Bible.

Jesus Makes Things

All things were made through him.
Nothing was made without him.

John 1:3

D o you like to make things? Do you like to paint or use crayons to color pictures? Have you ever drawn a picture to give to someone? Did they hang it up? Your parents probably hang up your drawings at home or maybe where they work. Children love to make things. Jesus loves to make things too. Jesus made everything. He made the world. He even made people. Jesus made you!

Jesus, thank You for making everything and everyone. Thank You for making me.

Jesus makes everything.

Jesus Is the Way

Jesus answered, "I am the way. And
I am the truth and the life. The only
way to the Father is through me."

John 14:6

God loves you. He wants you to be His friend.
Do you know how to be God's friend? Jesus
came to show us how to be God's friend. Jesus is
the way to God. When we love Jesus and do the
things He tells us to do, we also love God. God is
Jesus' Father, and Jesus knows all about God. He
leads us to God, our Father in heaven.

Lord, thank You for sending Jesus to help me know God,
my Father in heaven.

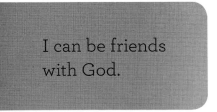

I can be friends
with God.

Dr. J. Kie Bowman, Hyde Park Baptist Church, Austin, TX

My Happy Life

There was hope that everything God made would have the freedom and glory that belong to God's children.
Romans 8:21

At your house, do you open presents on Christmas morning? It is fun to be together and give each other presents. God loves to give His children presents too. The presents God gives do not come on Christmas. God gives us gifts every day. He gives us family, friends, food to eat, and a home to live in. Most important, He gives us His Son, Jesus, so that we can be with Him forever. When you are God's friend, you can be happy because God loves you and He will always be with you.

Thank You, God, that I can be happy because I am with You. I want to be Your friend. I love You.

I can be happy because I know God.

Through the Valley

The Lord is my shepherd. I have everything I need.

Psalm 23:1

Have you ever had to walk somewhere kind of scary, like a street that was sort of dark? When David said, "The Lord is my shepherd," he was experiencing a scary time. But he knew that God would provide exactly what he needed to stay strong and show him where he needed to go. Maybe you are a little afraid of something. That is okay. But remember that God is always right beside you, even in the scariest times.

God, always remind me that when I am scared, You are right there beside me.

Jesus is always with you.

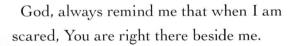

Caring for the Poor

God, in your goodness you took care
of the poor.

Psalm 68:10

There are people in your city and state and all over the world who do not have enough food to eat or a home to live in. That makes God very sad. He does not want people to be hungry and homeless. The Bible says that we should show His love to people by taking care of them and their needs. What can you do today to help the poor people who live in your town? What about the poor people on the other side of the world? Ask your parents to help you think of ways you can give to those who have less than you. God will be so happy when you show His love by caring for them.

God, show me how to help those who are poor. I want to show them Your love.

Caring for those who are poor is one of the best ways we can show we love Jesus.

Teacher's Pet

My child, do not forget my teaching.
Keep my commands in mind.

Proverbs 3:1

Have you ever known a teacher's pet? That means someone is the teacher's favorite student. Have you ever been the teacher's pet? The truth is, most teachers have a lot of children who are special to them. Teachers are happy with their students when they remember what to do and follow instructions. They want their students to be kind and learn and obey the rules. Be kind to your teachers. They want what is best for you, and the things they teach you are important.

Thank You, God, for caring enough about me to show me how to follow Your Word.

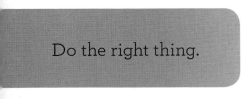

Do the right thing.

A Long Life with Jesus

My child, listen and accept what I say. Then you will have a long life.

Proverbs 4:10

God wants us listen to Him and to be strong and honest. God tells us everything we need to know in the Bible to lead a good life that makes Him happy. Listen to your parents, pastors, and Sunday school teachers when they tell you about God. As you learn more about Him, you will receive His promises and blessings.

Dear God, help me listen to You so that I will know what You want me to do.

Listen to God and do what He says.

Give to God

Honor the Lord by giving him part of your wealth.

Proverbs 3:9

Do your parents give you an allowance, or do you earn money by doing chores around the house? The money you receive is a blessing from God. It is important to thank Him. The Bible says that we honor God when we give Him part of the money that we have. You can add your money to the collection plate at church or ask your parents to help you give money to people who do not know about God. It will make you happy to help others, and it will make God happy too!

Thank You for everything You have given me, God. I want to give some back to You and Your church so everyone can know the story of Jesus.

Always give generously.

The Kingdom of God

"The thing you should want most is God's kingdom and doing what God wants."

Matthew 6:33

H ave you ever played hide-and-seek? It is fun to find such a good hiding place that your friends cannot find you. But Jesus says the most important thing to find is really easy to find. If we look for His kingdom, He will show it to us. This kingdom is not hard to find. It is all around us, if only we will look, because God's love is with us always. We do not have to play hide-and-seek with Jesus. We only have to ask, and He will help us find everything we need.

Thank You, God, for showing me Your kingdom. I pray that I will always put You first.

God's kingdom is easy to find, but you have to look for it.

"I Do Not Understand"

"I will send you the Helper from the Father. He is the Spirit of truth who comes from the Father."

John 15:26

Jesus taught others by telling stories. Sometimes His friends did not understand everything He taught. They had lots of questions for Jesus. They wanted answers before He had to go away. How would they know what was true without Him?

Jesus knew what they needed. He sent the Holy Spirit to help them. The Spirit helped them tell everyone about Jesus. The Holy Spirit will help you understand the truth about Jesus. Then you can teach your friends about Him too.

Jesus, I know You taught amazing things. Thank You for helping me understand. I will tell others what I learn.

God's Spirit helps me know His truth and share it.

Derek Jones, The People's Church, Franklin, TN

Not Alone

"When I go away I will send the Helper to you."

John 16:7

When Jesus was on the earth, He taught His friends how to trust Him and love others. But now it was time to say good-bye. His friends were scared about what would happen next. Jesus promised to send help. Jesus' friends trusted Him. With Jesus' help, they shared God's love to the whole world! Sometimes doing things by yourself is scary. But Jesus is a friend you can trust. He always keeps His promises. When you feel alone and nervous, you can talk to Jesus. He will help you too!

Jesus, thank You for being a friend I can trust. I know You help me when I feel alone.

I can trust Jesus to help me.

Braver Together

I will not be afraid because the Lord is with me.

Psalm 118:6

Sometimes bad things can happen. You may not understand why someone is mean to you. You may not know why someone has to move away. Many things can make you feel afraid. When you are worried, Jesus will help you. Things can be much less scary when someone is with you. Even when the people you love and trust cannot be around, Jesus will help you be brave. He will help you by always being with you.

Jesus, I know You love me even when bad things happen. Help me remember You are with me when I am afraid.

With God, I can be brave.

Go for It!

"When the Helper comes, he will prove to the people of the world the truth about sin, about being right with God, and about judgment."

John 16:8

God wants everyone to know about His love and forgiveness. Jesus came to make things right with God and His people. The Helper came after Jesus went back to heaven so everyone can know God's huge love. We are part of God's plan to share His friendship with everyone we know. The Helper will give you the courage to speak and the words to say. God sent His Helper so we can point others to Him. God loves you. God loves the whole world. With the Helper, you can tell everyone about God.

Jesus, thank You for bringing forgiveness to the world. Help me share God's love and friendship everywhere I go.

God loves you. God forgives you. Tell everybody!

Do You Remember?

"But the Helper will teach you everything. He will cause you to remember all the things I told you."
John 14:26

Jesus' friends did not understand where He was going or why He had to leave. Jesus sent the Helper so they could remember His plan. They had to tell the world everything Jesus taught. The Holy Spirit was with them when they were sad and helped them remember Jesus' lessons.

Have you ever had a big change in your life? It can be scary. The Helper brings peace when big things change around you. He will help you remember things you were taught about Jesus. He will be with you so you do not have to be afraid.

Jesus, I know Your Helper is with me even when things change. Help me remember Your lessons when I do not know Your plan.

The Helper brings hope when things change.

Derek Jones, The People's Church, Franklin, TN

Better Together

Also, the Spirit helps us. We are
very weak, but the Spirit helps us
with our weakness.

Romans 8:26

Are there things you cannot do by yourself or
do not know how to do? When you want to
reach something high, fix broken stuff, or learn
a new skill, you need to ask for help. Parents,
teachers, and coaches are around to help you. With
their help, you learn what to do.
When we do not know what to
do in life, God's Spirit will help
us. You might need help with
being kind, obedient, or patient.
Even if you do not know the words to
pray, God's Spirit will help you.

Jesus, thank You for sending Your
Spirit to help me. I know You love me and
have a good plan for my life.

I can trust God's Spirit
when I need help.

Believe in Me

Jesus said, "Don't let your hearts be troubled. Trust in God. And trust in me."

John 14:1

Jesus is saying that God loves you! Do not let things bother you. Do not worry. Believe that He loves you. Trust Him to take care of you. When you do not understand things that are happening to you, remember that He is with you. You cannot always feel God with you, so you have to remember the truth that He is there. The Bible says that God loves you! He will take care of everything.

Thank You, Lord, for giving me feelings. Help me remember that it is not about how I feel but what I know is true. Help me always remember how much You love me.

I know that God loves me!

God Keeps His Promise

Abraham waited patiently for this to happen.
And he received what God promised.

Hebrews 6:15

God promised Abraham that he would have as many children and grandchildren and great-grandchildren and so on as there are stars! That is a lot of people! God said that He would bless all those people and make them into a great nation. Abraham was seventy-five years old. He had no children. But he believed God's promise and followed God's Word. God kept His promise. Twenty-five years later, Abraham's son Isaac was born. Sometimes it is hard to wait, but God's best is worth waiting for. Remember, God is always on time. He is never late.

Lord, thank You for loving me and wanting the best for me. Help me wait on Your timing. Thank You for wanting the best for my life.

God always keeps His promises.

He Is Faithful

Depend on the Lord. Trust him, and he will take care of you.

Psalm 37:5

Do you know what God's favorite name is? Father! To be a father, you have to have a family, and we are the children of God. Just like your mom and dad love, feed, clothe, and protect you, God wants you to know that you can count on Him to take care of you. You are never out of His sight. He is always there and will never leave you.

Lord, thank You for always being there. Thank You for taking care of me. Help me always remember how much You love me.

God said He will take care of me.

The Bible

All Scripture is given by God and is
useful for teaching.

2 Timothy 3:16

Have you ever drawn a card for your mom
and dad to tell them how much you love
them? The Bible is God's love letter written to
His children. It contains great truths to live by. It
contains wisdom to help us make right decisions. It
tells us He created us and wants us to be with Him
in heaven forever. The Bible is the story of Jesus.
God gave us His Word so we can know Him. We
read the Bible to grow, learn, and know
God's truth.

Lord, thank You for the Bible. Thank
You that You want me to know You and
You want to help me learn about You.

The Bible is God's love
letter written to me.

A Special Promise

We know that in everything God works for the good of those who love him.

Romans 8:28

Everything that happens in life is not always good. There are bad people who do bad things. Things do not always go the way you want them to. The good news is God has a plan for your life. God has a purpose for you. Because He loves you, He works everything together for your good. Nothing can stop His plan.

Jesus, help me remember You are in control. Help me keep my eyes on You and never forget You have a plan for my life.

Jesus has a plan and purpose for my life.

Having Faith

So people receive God's promise by
having faith. This happens so that
the promise can be a free gift.

Romans 4:16

Faith is taking God at His Word. It is believing
what God promises. God says He loves you
and will never leave you. He says He will take care
of you. He says He has a plan for your life. Do you
believe what God is saying? Not with your head,
but with your heart? You cannot see the air around
you, but you know that it is there. That is faith.

Jesus, thank You for all the promises You have given me.
Help me believe in my heart what You have promised.

> Faith is believing
> what God says.

Jesus Makes a Promise

You have this faith and love because of your hope, and what you hope for is saved for you in heaven.

Colossians 1:5

When Jesus makes us a promise, we can always count on Him keeping it. When He tells us something, we can believe that He is telling us the truth. Jesus promises us that if we love Him and ask Him to forgive us, we will be with Him in heaven forever. You can trust that is true because Jesus is perfect, and He always keeps His promises.

Dear Jesus, thank You for loving me and saving me a place in heaven right beside You. I love You, Jesus!

Jesus always keeps His promises!

Tim Anderson, Clements Baptist Church, Athens, AL

Jumping for Joy

"I tell you there is much joy in heaven when 1 sinner changes his heart."

Luke 15:7

Have you ever sung the song: "I got the joy, joy, joy, joy, down in my heart. Where? Down in my heart. Where? Down in my heart. I got the joy, joy, joy, joy, down in my heart. Down in my heart to stay." When you are feeling sad, ask Jesus to be your best friend. He will love you and never leave you. Heaven is always happy when we change our heart and allow Jesus to love us.

Dear Jesus, thank You for loving me and for being my best friend.

Jesus loves you and wants to be your best friend.

Bread of Heaven

"My Father gives you the true bread from heaven."

John 6:32

Jesus said that He is the bread of heaven. Our bodies need food to keep us healthy, and we need Jesus to take away our sins so we can live forever with Him. God gave us Jesus so that we would have everything we need. Heaven is a place filled with good things. Jesus is there, and one day we can be with Him if we love Him and believe in Him.

Dear God, thank You for giving us Jesus.

Jesus is all you need.

True Treasure

"So store your treasure in heaven. The treasures in heaven cannot be destroyed by moths or rust."
Matthew 6:20

D o you have a piggy bank where you keep your money or a box where you put the things that are very important to you? We have lots of things that are special to us on earth, but those things can get broken or lost. When you spend your money, it is gone. When we get to heaven, we will have good things like love and happiness and most importantly, Jesus. Those things will be with us forever. We can enjoy all the blessings that God gives us now, but remember that God's love will last forever.

Dear Jesus, thank You for all of my blessings. Help me remember that loving You and serving You are what is most important.

Jesus will be with us forever.

My Name Makes Me Happy

"You should be happy because your names are written in heaven."

Luke 10:20

It is exciting when you learn how to write your name. When we ask Jesus to become our best friend, the Bible says He writes our name in heaven right beside His name, and no one will ever take it away. Jesus loves you, and nothing you say or do will ever change that. Your name is written in heaven, and He has made a special place for you there so you can be with Him forever.

Dear Jesus, thank You for writing my name beside Your name in heaven.

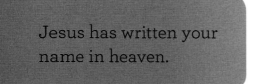

Jesus has written your name in heaven.

Tim Anderson, Clements Baptist Church, Athens, AL

Be Happy

"Rejoice and be glad. You have a great reward waiting for you in heaven."

Matthew 5:12

It is fun to get a reward. Our parents often tell us that we can earn a reward from them if we work hard and do our jobs at home. When we do what our parents tell us to do, it makes them happy and we are rewarded for it. One day Jesus will reward us for obeying Him. Loving Jesus and obeying Him are the most important things we can ever do in life.

Dear Jesus, thank You for loving me and giving me a reward in heaven. I love You, Jesus.

Obeying Jesus brings rewards in heaven and makes Jesus smile.

Shine Bright

"You are the light that gives light to the world. A city that is built on a hill cannot be hidden."

Matthew 5:14

Have you ever played with a flashlight? If the batteries are not good, then the light will not shine. It only shines bright when you put in new batteries and turn it on. Just like good batteries inside a flashlight make the flashlight shine, Jesus wants you and me to let Him shine in our lives. How? By letting the love of Jesus be the batteries in us. His love helps us shine brighter. Just like a flashlight needs good batteries, we need the love of Jesus.

Jesus, I'm glad You love me. Thank You for shining Your love in my life so my life can shine.

The love of Jesus shines bright for everyone.

Give Kindness

"In the same way, you should be a light for other people. Live so that they will see the good things you do."

Matthew 5:16

When we do good things for others, God's love shines through us. Today, do something good for someone. Hold a door open for a friend. Smile at a teacher who looks like she is having a bad day. Offer to help your mom or dad clean up the kitchen after dinner. By being kind to others, we are like sunshine after a rain storm. We can be the sunshine in someone's life by being kind to them.

Jesus, today may I be kind to others and help them know how special they are.

Kindness is a gift we give away to our friends.

See Good

"The eye is a light for the body. If your eyes are good, then your whole body will be full of light."

Matthew 6:22

Jesus wants us look at things that are beautiful and good. It makes God happy when we look at the stars in the sky, play with our friends, or read books about Jesus. We feel good when we enjoy things that we know God loves. The Bible says that when we look at things that God says are good, it fills us with goodness and light. Just like the moon makes the night bright, the love of Jesus makes our lives bright and happy.

Jesus, thank You for Your love that makes me happy.

The love of Jesus is shining upon you.

Tim DeTellis, New Missions, Orlando, FL

Bright Love

"If your whole body is full of light,
and none of it is dark, then you will
shine bright, as when a lamp shines
on you."

Luke 11:36

Have you ever woken up early enough to watch
the sun rise? It can feel a little cold before the
sun comes up because it is still dark outside. Then,
when the sun rises, the world begins to shine and
you can feel the sun's warmth. Just like the sun
shines on us when we are outside, God's love is
always shining on us and warming us up.

Thank You, Jesus, for loving me today.
Every day when the sun rises, I will
remember You love me.

Your love shining on me
is like a gift from heaven.

Our Friend Jesus

"Believe in the light while you still have it. Then you will become sons of light."

John 12:36

Jesus was not going to be on the earth much longer. He wanted His disciples to enjoy spending time with Him. And He wanted them to know that even after He was gone, He would be with them. Jesus is always with us. We can talk to Him anytime. His love makes us feel warm and happy. When we feel Jesus' love, we shine bright enough for others to see His love too!

Thank You, Jesus, for being close to me no matter where I am. I believe You are with me each day.

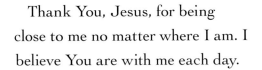

Jesus is always with us.

Good-bye Darkness

"I have come as light into the world.
I came so that whoever believes in
me would not stay in darkness."
John 12:46

Have the lights ever gone out in your house at night during a storm? That can be kind of scary because you cannot see well. Your mom or dad probably got out a flashlight or lit some candles. The light chased the darkness away, and you could see things around you. Jesus came into the world to chase away things that make you afraid. He shines His light of love and forgiveness and makes everything better.

Dear Jesus, I want You to be my best friend and stay with me even when storms come.

Jesus is with you no matter where you go.

Ask Jesus for Help

"Continue to ask, and God will give to you."

Matthew 7:7

Jesus said to ask Him for anything. Do you need help with your math problems or vocabulary words? Ask Jesus to help you learn and study. Do you have a game or recital coming up? Ask Jesus, and He will help you practice so you can do your best. Is somebody annoying or bothering you? Ask Jesus to help you show love to them. Remember to ask Jesus for help. He will give you what you need.

Jesus, I need You. Thank You helping me when I ask.

Jesus wants me to ask Him to help me.

Pastor Scott and Leslie Yirka,
Hibernia Baptist Church, Fleming Island, FL

What Can I Do?

"Without me he can do nothing."
John 15:5

What are some ways a follower of Jesus should act? Should followers of Jesus be obedient to their parents and teachers? Should they be kind to other people? Should they always be truthful? What else should followers of Jesus be?

Jesus told us that without Him, we could not do anything that pleases Him. We need Jesus to help us be like Him. We cannot do it by ourselves.

Jesus, I know I cannot do what pleases You without You. Please continue to make me like You in every way.

We can do what pleases Jesus only because Jesus is in us.

Jesus Forgives

He is our great hope, and he will
come with glory.

Titus 2:13

D o you get excited when company is coming to
your house? It is so much fun when friends or
grandparents visit. Do you start looking for them
when it is time for them to arrive? Chances are, you
look out the window or stand outside waiting. Jesus
said He is coming back one day soon. We do not
know when He is coming, but it could be today!

Jesus, You promised You would come back. Help me be
ready for You when You come back.

Jesus is coming back.

Guess Who Prayed for You?

"I pray for them now. . . . I am praying for those men you gave me, because they are yours."

John 17:9

It is wonderful when someone prays for us. Did you know someone very special prayed for you? Jesus prayed for you, and He still does (see Hebrews 7:25). Jesus prayed that you would believe in Him and love Him. Remember when you say your prayers to Jesus that He has prayed for you and still does.

Jesus, thank You for praying for me. I know no one cares about me as much as You do.

Jesus prayed for you.

Pastor Scott and Leslie Yirka,
Hibernia Baptist Church, Fleming Island, FL

You Can Tell Others About Jesus

During the night, Paul had a vision. The Lord said to him, "Don't be afraid! Continue talking to people and don't be quiet!"

Acts 18:9

S hhh! *Be quiet.* Can you think of some places where you have to be really quiet? It can be hard to be quiet sometimes. But there are also places where you get to talk and have fun being loud. There is a time to be quiet, and there is a time not to be, isn't there?

In Acts 18, Jesus told Paul not to be quiet about Him. Everyone needs to know about Jesus. Did you know that Jesus does not want you to be quiet about Him? Do not be afraid to tell others about Jesus.

Jesus, help me not be afraid to tell others about You today and every day.

I will tell others about Jesus.

Pastor Scott and Leslie Yirka,
Hibernia Baptist Church, Fleming Island, FL

Who Can You Pray For?

"I pray for these men. But I am also praying for all people who will believe in me because of the teaching of these men."

John 17:20

You can be like Jesus by praying for others. Can you pray for your mom and dad? How about your brothers and sisters? Do you know someone who is sick? Do you have a friend who needs to know about Jesus? Can you pray for your pastor? Who else can you pray for? Jesus took time to pray for others. Take some time to pray for other people now.

Jesus, thank You that I can pray for others who need Your help or need to know about You.

You can pray for others like Jesus did.

God Is My Friend

So don't worry, because I am with you. Don't be afraid, because I am your God.

Isaiah 41:10

God told us not to be afraid, but sometimes that's hard to do. God says we don't have to be scared because He is with us all the time. We don't see Him and we don't hear Him, but He watches over us from heaven. God is our friend. When we feel afraid, He wants us to know that He cares about us and He is always with us.

Dear God, thank You for being my friend. I know You are there when I feel afraid. I love You, God.

God watches over me.

God's Love Is Good

Where God's love is, there is no fear,
because God's perfect love takes
away fear.

1 John 4:18

There are many things that we love. We love
our mom and dad. We love our cats and dogs.
Love is a feeling we have inside our heart. Love
is wonderful, but God's love is even better. Long
ago, God sent Jesus down from heaven to show us
His love. God's love is with us, and we do not need
to be afraid. We don't have to worry because God
loves us.

Thank You, Jesus, for coming down to show us God's
love. I love You, Jesus.

God sent Jesus to show
us how to love.

Be Strong and Brave

All you who put your hope in the
Lord be strong and brave.

Psalm 31:24

In a land far away, a long, long time ago, there
lived a good king named David. He was very
strong and brave. Since David loved God with all
his heart, he wanted to make God happy. He tried
to obey God and trusted that God loved him. David
knew that God was with him every day, so he did
not have to be afraid. God is always with us too.

God, help me be strong and brave. I know that You will
be with me every day.

God wants us to be
strong and brave.

Waiting for God

Wait for the Lord's help. Be strong
and brave and wait for the Lord's
help.

Psalm 27:14

It is not easy to wait for something that we
want with all our hearts. It is hard to wait for
Christmas morning or our birthday, but when those
days finally get here—wow! It's great! God told
us to wait for His help. We may feel upset about
something, but if we ask for the Lord's help, He
will help us. Sometimes we just have to wait.

Lord, I know You will help me when I need
Your help. Make me strong and brave so
that I can wait for Your help.

God will always
help us.

Don't Be Afraid

Jesus quickly spoke to them. He said, "Have courage! It is I! Don't be afraid."

Matthew 14:27

Jesus had twelve men who helped Him tell people about God. They were called disciples. One day, Jesus told His disciples to get into their boat and go to the other side of the lake. The disciples worked hard to get the boat to the other shore. Suddenly they saw someone walking on the water coming toward them. They were scared. Then they saw it was Jesus walking on the water. Jesus told them not to be afraid.

Jesus, I'm afraid sometimes. Please be with me when I'm scared.

Jesus is with us even when we are scared.

Do Not Be Shy

God did not give us a spirit that makes us afraid. He gave us a spirit of power and love and self-control.

2 Timothy 1:7

A long time ago, there was a young man named Timothy who was very shy. Timothy loved Jesus, but he was afraid to tell people about Him. One day, a preacher named Paul told him that God would help him be brave to talk to others, and after that, Timothy was not shy and told everyone about Jesus.

Jesus, my friends need to know You. Help me tell them about You. Please help me know what to say.

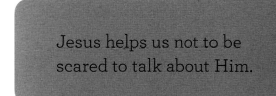

Jesus helps us not to be scared to talk about Him.

Thinking About God Makes Him Happy

> "Those who are pure in their thinking are happy."
>
> Matthew 5:8

When you think about God and the good things He has done, that makes Him happy. The Bible says we are blessed when we think about God and read the Bible every day. Do you think about God often? When you think about God, think about how caring He is and how much He loves you. Thinking about God and what the Bible says will make you happy!

God, help me think about You and all the great things You have done.

My thoughts can make me and God happy.

Dr. Zach Zettler, First Baptist Jackson, Jackson, MS

Read the Bible Every Day

Keep yourself pure.

1 Timothy 5:22

It is important to read the Bible every day. The Bible tells you how to be like Jesus, and it helps you do the right thing. Reading the Bible may not be easy, but it is important! The Bible is full of real and exciting stories of God's love for everyone, especially you. When you read the Bible, it helps you grow up to be more like Jesus. Remember that God is always with you and will help you make good choices and do the things that please Him.

God, help me find time to read my Bible every day.

I can read the Bible every day.

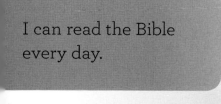

Be Like Jesus

Christ is pure. And every person who has this hope in Christ keeps himself pure like Christ.

1 John 3:3

Jesus was the only perfect person who ever lived! That is what it means to be pure. Everything He did was good and right. He never had a bad thought or said a mean thing. The Bible says that we are supposed to be like Jesus. God knows that we cannot be perfect. That is why we need Jesus. But He does want us to try our best to think good thoughts, say kind words, and be loving to others. Ask God to help you love others the way Jesus does.

God, I want to be like Jesus. Help me be kind and loving and make good choices.

God wants us to be like Jesus.

Being Kind

To those who are pure, all things are
pure.

Titus 1:15

When we follow God, we want everything we do to make Him happy. You probably have a favorite toy, but sometimes your friend might want to play with it. God wants you to learn to share your things with others. You can also make God happy when you use polite words when you ask for things or answer a question. God wants you to be kind when talking with others. We show God we love Him when we try to be like Him in everything we say and do.

God, help me be like You in everything I do.

Be kind always.

Trust God

Let us come near to God with a
sincere heart and a sure faith.
Hebrews 10:22

God promises to love you always. He wants you to trust that everything He has said in the Bible is true. Trusting God and believing in Him is having a sure faith. God wants you to tell Him all the things that you think and feel. He wants you to be honest with Him. You have a sincere heart when you tell God the truth. God loves you, and He knows all about you. You can trust that He will never leave you and will love you no matter what!

God, thank You for always being near me and loving me. Help me trust You and be honest with You.

I can tell God anything because I know that He loves me.

Dr. Zach Zettler, First Baptist Jackson, Jackson, MS

Pleasing God

But the wisdom that comes from
God is like this: First, it is pure.
Then it is also peaceful, gentle, and
easy to please.

James 3:17

Jesus was kind and gentle and loved everyone.
God wants us to be kind and gentle too. You
can be peaceful when you choose not to fight with
your friend but instead let her go first when you are
playing a game. When your parents ask you to do
something, being easy to please means that you do
it quickly and with a good attitude. God wants you
to learn to do what is asked of you and be
loving to others.

God, help me be
gentle and please You in
everything I do.

I want to please
God.

A Giving Heart

"Give, and you will receive. . . . The way you give to others is the way God will give to you."

Luke 6:38

It makes God very happy when we give our time and things to others to help them. What can you do for people who might have less than you? Maybe you can give some of your stuffed animals to a children's hospital. Or maybe you can have a lemonade stand and send the money to a country that has had a natural disaster. There are so many ways you can help others. Giving pleases God, and it will make your heart happy too!

God, help me do what I can do to help others. Help me enjoy sharing what You have given me.

God has a giving heart, and it makes Him happy when we give.

Always Love and Be Kind

Love is patient and kind. Love is not jealous, it does not brag, and it is not proud.

1 Corinthians 13:4

The Bible tells us over and over again how much God loves us. He loves everyone, even if they do not love Him back. He loves you so much. He thinks you are very special! You should always love others and be kind to them. It makes people feel sad if you are rude or do not treat them nicely. Always show God's love to others and be kind.

Dear Jesus, help me love everyone like You do, even if they are not always nice to me.

God's love is very special, and He will always love you!

Forgive Like Jesus

Be kind and loving to each other. Forgive each other just as God forgave you in Christ.

Ephesians 4:32

The Bible teaches that we all do bad things. Maybe you have told a lie or disobeyed your parents. The Bible says that when you do these things, you should pray and ask God to forgive you. And He does! He loves you, and He forgives you for what you have done. God always forgives us, so it makes Him very happy when we forgive those who do something wrong to us. Is there someone you need to forgive today?

God, thank You for forgiving me when I do wrong. Help me forgive others the way You have forgiven me.

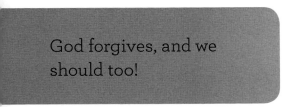

God forgives, and we should too!

Pastor Steve Flockhart, New Season Church, Hiram, GA

Friends Are a Gift

Love each other like brothers and sisters.
Give your brothers and sisters more
honor than you want for yourselves.
Romans 12:10

D o you enjoy spending time with your friends?
Sometimes you wish they could stay at your
house all the time! Sometimes you spend so much
time with your friends that they seem like your
brothers and sisters. We should love our friends.
We should say nice things to them, let them play
with our favorite toys, let them choose what game
to play, and pray for them. Be a good friend today!

Dear God, thank You for giving
me good friends. Help me have
fun times with all of my
friends.

Friends are a gift
from God.

I Can Teach Others

She speaks wise words. And she
teaches others to be kind.

Proverbs 31:26

It is important to God that we are kind. He
wants us to be kind, and He also wants us to
teach others to be kind. If you see boys or girls
being mean to someone or not playing with
that person, you should be kind and be
their friend. The other kids will see how
important it is to be nice. You can be the
one who is kind, and others will watch you
and act the same.

Dear God, help me be kind to everyone
and teach others to do the same.

I can be an example
of God's love.

Add a Little Love and Kindness

Add kindness for your brothers and sisters
in Christ; and to this kindness, add love.
2 Peter 1:7

When your mom makes a cake, she mixes eggs, butter, sugar, and other yummy things together. After the cake bakes, she adds sweet frosting to the top. Then you get to eat a delicious cake!

We can add things to our life to make it better, just like the frosting on the cake makes it even yummier. Two things that we can add are kindness and love. This makes our parents happy and our family, friends, and teachers happy. It makes God happy. It also makes us happy because we are doing the right thing.

Dear God, help me add kindness and love to my life every day.

If we add God's love and kindness to our life, it makes our life better.

Pastor Steve Flockhart, New Season Church, Hiram, GA

Helping People
I Love

Serve each other with love.

Galatians 5:13

Your mom and dad do a lot of things for you. They pack your lunch, wash your clothes, and help you with your homework. Why do you think they do all these special things for you? It is because they love you very much. When you love people, you want to take care of them and help them have a happy day and make them smile. Jesus did this too. We can please Jesus when we do things for our family, our friends, and our neighbors. What can you do to help others and be like Jesus?

Dear God, help me be kind and help people when they need it.

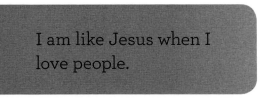

I am like Jesus when I love people.

Dr. Ted Traylor, Olive Baptist Church, Pensacola, FL

When Someone Is Sad

Help each other with your troubles.
Galatians 6:2

When people you care about are sad, you want to make them feel better. Maybe you could give them a picture you have colored. If you want to make them laugh, you could tell them a joke. One of the best things you can do is give them a big hug and say, "I love you." And do not forget to pray for them, because God can make all things better.

Jesus was very kind to people who were hurting. He made them feel special and loved. He wants us to do that for others too! Think of someone who was sad today. How can you be kind and help them?

Dear God, please show me ways to help others when they are sad.

I can comfort someone who is sad.

Jesus Can Help Us Love Others

Love each other deeply with all your heart.
1 Peter 1:22

It is easy to love someone who is nice and does things for you. But what about people who say unkind things or are mean? That is hard! People were mean to Jesus too. They did not like Him, so they made a plan to kill Him. But no matter what others did to Him, Jesus loved them with all His heart and even died for their sins.

When we are mean back to a person, it just makes things worse. Jesus wants us to love others by showing them kindness. It is not always easy, but with His help, we can do it.

Dear God, help me be kind to everyone.

Be kind to show Jesus' love.

Thank You for Sunday Workers

We should give special attention to those who are in the family of believers.
Galatians 6:10

Sunday morning is a special time because people who love God get to be together at church! Many people have been working all week to get ready for you. Your Sunday school teacher studied the Bible story to share with you. Helpers got all the crafts ready for you to make. It was someone's job to make sure you have yummy snacks too! Being grateful to people who serve us is very important. The next time you go to church, remember to thank someone for making church a special place to be.

Dear God, thank You for everyone who helps me grow to be like Jesus.

Tell your Sunday school teacher or pastor thank you on Sunday.

How Can I Help People?

Be good servants and use your gifts to serve each other.

1 Peter 4:10

Did you know God made you special and there is no one else like you? It is true! Even your fingerprints are different from anyone else's who has ever lived. God also created us to enjoy different ways of serving Him. Do you like to sing? People would love to hear you praise God with your voice. Do you like to meet people? You can welcome new friends to your Sunday school class. Do you like to be a helper? You can clean up after making crafts or eating snacks. There are lots of ways you can use your gifts to please God.

Dear God, I want to use my gifts to help others.

I can serve God by helping at church.

Dr. Ted Traylor, Olive Baptist Church, Pensacola, FL

How Can I Be Like Christ?

To be like Christ, a person must do what is right.

1 John 3:7

Every day you make a lot of choices. Some choices are good, such as sharing your toys. Other choices can get you in trouble, like doing something your mom and dad said not to do. When we make a choice to obey, this makes God happy. When we listen to Him and do the right thing, we feel good inside. The more right choices we make, the more we are like Jesus. We think like Him and act like Him and want to please Him.

Dear God, please help me make good decisions and want to be like You.

I want to be like Jesus.

Do What Is Right

Lord, teach me your ways. Guide me
to do what is right.

Psalm 27:11

The Bible tells us the right things to do, like
obeying, being kind, and telling the truth. Can
you think of other right things to do? Choosing to
do right is not always easy. Sometimes you may
think your friends will laugh at you if you choose
to do the right thing. Even if no one sees you, it
is important to do the right thing. God is pleased
when you make a good choice, and He can give
you courage to do it.

Thank You, God, that the Bible tells
me what is right. Help me make right
choices, even when it is not easy.

God helps me do the
right thing.

Do Not Worry

Give all your worries to him,
because he cares for you.

1 Peter 5:7

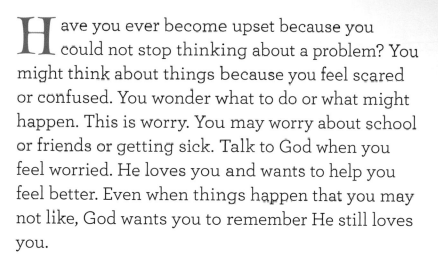

Have you ever become upset because you could not stop thinking about a problem? You might think about things because you feel scared or confused. You wonder what to do or what might happen. This is worry. You may worry about school or friends or getting sick. Talk to God when you feel worried. He loves you and wants to help you feel better. Even when things happen that you may not like, God wants you to remember He still loves you.

Dear God, thank You that I can tell you when I am worried and I know You will listen. Help me think about how much You care about me.

When I feel worried, I should pray.

Help Others

The person who serves should serve
with the strength that God gives.

1 Peter 4:11

To serve means to help someone or to do something nice for someone. When you serve others, you should think about them more than you think about yourself. Serve someone to show them you love them. When you help others, it also shows them you love God. Sometimes serving is hard work; sometimes it is fun work. God can give you energy to help others. What are some ways you can serve your family, friends, neighbors, or church?

God, please give me ideas for serving people. Remind me to think about others and how much You love them.

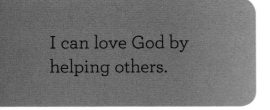

I can love God by
helping others.

Kim Williams, First Baptist Woodstock, Woodstock, GA

Think About Others

Encourage each other every day.
Hebrews 3:13

Have you ever had a friend who felt sad, lonely, left out, embarrassed, or tired? The Bible says we are to encourage people when they feel this way. This means we try to help them feel better. There are many ways to encourage your friends. You can smile at them, listen to them, talk to them, or play with them. What are other ways to encourage someone?

Lord, help me realize when I should encourage someone around me. Thank You for the people who encourage me too.

Think about someone to encourage today.

Honor Others

Be humble and give more honor to others than to yourselves.

Philippians 2:3

Saying kind things about someone else is a nice thing to do. Playing what someone else wants to play instead of what you want to play is kind. Obeying your parents is right. Wanting good things to happen to other people is unselfish. When you behave this way toward others, you are honoring them. When you honor others, you are also honoring God.

Dear God, help me be unselfish and honor people more. Help me show others I love You by how I treat them.

I can honor people by what I do.

Think About Others

Be interested in the lives of others.
Philippians 2:4

Sometimes we get so busy thinking about the things we do or the things we care about that we forget to think about others. The Bible tells us we should let others know they are special. Show people you care by asking questions about their day or how they feel about things. Do something special for someone. Listen to friends and family when they want to talk to you. Tell people God loves them. These kinds of things can help people feel happy and special.

Jesus, help me let someone know that I am thinking about them today and that You love them.

Say something kind to someone today.

Helping Hands

"I have chosen you to be my servant.
You will be my witness."

Acts 26:16

Another word for *servant* is *helper*. Being a helper can be fun. Helping others shows them they are special and important to you and to God. Think of all the ways you can use your hands and feet to help or serve others. You might use your hands to pick up trash and use your feet to go tell others about God's amazing love. Being a helper is a special way to tell others about God and show them how much He loves them.

Jesus, help me use my hands and feet so that people will see how much You love them.

Helping others is a way to show God's love.

Analisa Hood & Suzanne Walker,
Mobberly Baptist Church, Longview, TX

Show and Tell

"Whoever accepts anyone I send also accepts me. And whoever accepts me also accepts the One who sent me."
John 13:20

God wants us to help others know Jesus. When we talk about Jesus and show kindness, love, and forgiveness, we help our family and friends learn more about who Jesus is. Knowing about Jesus helps people choose Him to be the Leader of their lives. Do you know someone who needs to know more about Jesus? What will you say or do to help someone know Jesus today?

Jesus, help me be ready to show and tell others about You.

I can tell others about Jesus.

Give It Your All

In all the work you are doing, work the best you can.

Colossians 3:23

Think about working as hard as you can at something you enjoy, like riding your bike or playing sports. Working hard at what you enjoy is easy to do. Now think about working as hard as you can at something you do not enjoy, like cleaning your room. This time doing your best might not be easy. Jesus wants you to always try your hardest and do the best job you can do. This pleases God.

Jesus, help me always give my best for You in everything I do.

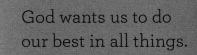

God wants us to do our best in all things.

Kings and Queens

It is true that serving God makes
a person very rich, if he is satisfied
with what he has.

1 Timothy 6:6

Would you like to be a king or queen?
Everyone would **serve** you and you would be
rich! God says we will be happier than kings and
queens if we serve Him instead of being served.
When we serve God, He makes us rich with His
love. That is the very best kind of rich to be! God
makes us so rich with love we can share it with
everyone and still have enough to be happy and
satisfied every day!

Jesus, help me want to serve God and others instead of
wanting others to serve me.

God's love is all I need.

Analisa Hood & Suzanne Walker,
Mobberly Baptist Church, Longview, TX

239

Power Up

And God is the One who makes you and us strong in Christ.

2 Corinthians 1:21

Flex your muscles. Do they feel strong? Exercise makes your muscles strong. There is another way to be strong that is not about exercise and muscles. God says He will make you strong in a different way. God's strength helps you make wise choices, care for the needs of others, and share the wonderful story of Jesus. God's strength and power is stronger than any muscle could ever be. He shares His strength with us so we can help others know Jesus.

Jesus, give me strength and power to share Your love with others.

God gives us power
to share His love.

Analisa Hood & Suzanne Walker,
Mobberly Baptist Church, Longview, TX

Jesus Helps Me

Let all men see that you are gentle
and kind.

Philippians 4:5

A re you gentle and kind when you hold a baby
kitten or puppy? It is easy to be gentle and
kind then. But what should we do when we feel
angry and want to have our own way? Jesus wants
us to help others know about His love by showing
them our gentleness and kindness. So Jesus
promises to help us be kind to others when it is
hard.

Jesus, help me remember to ask You for
help when I do not feel kind or gentle
inside.

Jesus helps me
show His kindness.

Actions Matter

"You are the light that gives light to the world."

Matthew 5:14

We can do good things and be a light that points others to Jesus. The Bible says our actions speak louder than our words. Someone special may have told you that they love you. Then they may have showed it by caring about you, giving you hugs, or being a great friend. God wants us to show His love to others by being kind. How can you show someone that you love them today?

Dear God, please help me show Your love and be kind to others. I want to be a light for Jesus!

Actions speak louder than words.

Jesus' Helpers

"Whoever helps one of these little ones because they are my followers will truly get his reward."

Matthew 10:42

Being a follower of Jesus is important. God has given you parents and teachers and friends to help you because He loves you. When someone does something nice for you, you should thank them. And you should thank God.

Adults are not the only ones who can help others. There are so many things you can do. Think of ways that you can do kind things for others. God promises that He will bless you when you show His love. Maybe there is even someone younger than you, like a little brother or sister, that you can help today.

Dear God, thank You for those who help me learn about You. Help me help others too.

Even though I am young, I can help others.

Rev. Aaron Holloway, Burnt Hickory Baptist Church, Powder Springs, GA

Worry About Yourself

Each person must be responsible for himself.

Galatians 6:5

Sometimes we worry about what other people are doing wrong instead of thinking about what we are doing. God's Word tells us that we need to be responsible for our own actions. God wants us to make good choices, and He gave us the Bible to help us. Do you always tell the truth? Are you kind? Do you obey your parents? God wants us to obey His Word. He knows that we are not perfect and that we will make mistakes. When we do something wrong, we need to say we are sorry and ask for forgiveness.

Dear God, thank You for the Bible! Please help me keep my word and be responsible for my actions.

God says for you to be responsible for yourself.

Rev. Aaron Holloway, Burnt Hickory Baptist Church, Powder Springs, GA

Right Is Right

Don't let me be dishonest. Be kind to
me by helping me obey your teachings.

Psalm 119:29

God wants us to be honest and obey His Word.
Jesus reminds us to love everyone. We also
need to remember that right is always right. Wrong
is also always wrong. There are times that being
dishonest may be easier than telling the truth. But
God wants us to always do the right thing—even
when it is hard.

Dear God, thank You for Your Word.
Help me do the right thing and
obey Your Word.

God wants us to obey
Him and do right!

Honesty Matters

Good people will be guided by
honesty.

Proverbs 11:3

Good people believe being honest is important.
Has anyone ever lied to you? Was it hard to
trust the person who lied? What if that person has
lied over and over? Does it make trusting them
even harder? Most people trust others who tell the
truth and make good choices. God always tells the
truth. He wants us to be like Him, so we should be
honest and keep promises.

Dear God, thank You for keeping Your
promises and being trustworthy. Please
help me always tell the truth.

Telling the truth matters
if we want to obey God.

Speak the Truth

Never keep me from speaking your truth.

Psalm 119:43

God wants us to tell people the truth about Him. The Bible is His Word, and it is truth. We can share His Word with others by telling them about His goodness and about His Son, Jesus. There are others who have never heard about God or His Son. We can show how much we love Him by telling them about God and sharing His truth. By telling others about God, we will also show them how much we love them.

Dear God, thank You for Your truth! Help me look for ways to share Your Word and love with others.

> We can show God's love by telling the truth.

Rev. Aaron Holloway, Burnt Hickory Baptist Church, Powder Springs, GA

Star Light, Star Bright

Those who teach others to live right
will shine like stars forever and ever.
Daniel 12:3

Stars are wonderful to watch. They shimmer and shine for everyone to see. The Bible says that we can be like stars! God tells us that when we teach others to love and obey Him, we shine just as bright as the biggest star in the sky. When we teach our friends and family to be kind and good, our glow never goes away. Stars may one day lose their shine, but we never will.

Jesus, help me teach others to love and obey You. I want to shine bright for You.

I shine brightly when I teach others to love God.

Vance Pitman with Daniel Grothman,
Hope Church, Las Vegas, NV

Greatest Gift to Share

Jesus said to the followers, "Go everywhere in the world. Tell the Good News to everyone."

Mark 16:15

Have you ever been given a gift you loved so much that you had to tell everyone about it? We have been given the best gift anyone in the whole world could ever ask for . . . the gift of Jesus. He loves us and wants to be with us forever! This is the kind of gift worth telling others about. Share the good news of God's gift of Jesus to everyone in the world.

Lord, thank You for the gift of Jesus. Help me share the good news to everyone so they can receive the gift of Jesus too.

Jesus is worth talking about.

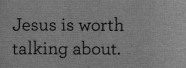

Love in Action

"You must love each other as I have loved you."

John 13:34

O ur world is huge, and it is filled with different cultures and people. Some think there may be as many as seven thousand languages! How will we be able to tell all those people about God's love for them? God knows that no matter what language we speak, we can show love to others through our actions. We can be an example of His love to everyone we meet.

Thank You, Jesus, for being the perfect example of our Father's love for us.

We can show God's love in how we live.

Kindness Brings Smiles

If one has the gift of showing kindness to others, that person should do so with joy.

Romans 12:8

God loves us so much He has given each of us gifts. One of those gifts is being kind. When we are kind to others, it brings a smile to their faces. There was once a paralyzed man. His friends showed him kindness and brought him to Jesus. Jesus healed the man, and he could walk again. He and his friends had so much joy. All of us can show kindness. When we do, it brings God joy.

God, please help me be kind to others, even when it can be hard. Help me have a kind heart.

We share God's love when we are kind.

Vance Pitman with Wes Hodges,
Hope Church, Las Vegas, NV

Glory to God

Live good lives. Then they will see the good things you do, and they will give glory to God.

1 Peter 2:12

God is so wonderful. He put the stars in the sky, sends cool breezes on hot summer days, and gives flowers their sweet smell. Because God is so amazing, He deserves our praise. The best way to praise God is to love and obey Him. The Bible tells us that when we obey God and do good, others will see us and give Him glory.

Jesus, help me obey God and do good so that others can see how wonderful You are and give You the glory.

When I obey God, others will praise Him.

252

Vance Pitman with Mike Mead,
Hope Church, Las Vegas, NV

God's Wisdom Is Perfect

[God's] wisdom is always ready to help those who are troubled and to do good for others. This wisdom is always fair and honest.

James 3:17

We can help our friends through hard times when we pray to God and ask for help. Sometimes we do not know why our friends are sad or hurting. Sometimes we do not know what to say. The best way to help is to ask God for wisdom and the words to say that will help make them feel better.

God, give me wisdom to help my friends when they are in trouble. Help me say words that are true and kind.

God gives wisdom to those who ask.

God Is Good

Give thanks to the Lord because he is good.

Psalm 136:1

God is good all the time! Everything He makes is good, and everything He does is good. You can trust Him because He has great plans for you, and He is in control of the world. Thank Him when you look around at all the good things He has made and the blessings He has given to you. Sing songs to Him and praise Him because He is good.

Thank You, God, for being perfect and good. Please help me be kind and good to other people, just like You are!

God is good!

Jesus Makes Me Happy

Always be happy. Never stop
praying. Give thanks whatever
happens.

1 Thessalonians 5:16–18

What makes you happy? Is it getting a new toy or a new game to play? Maybe it is going to your favorite place. Whatever it is that makes you happy, thank Jesus for it. Jesus wants us to be happy. He also wants us to talk to Him in prayer and tell Him thank You. When we thank Jesus, we are reminded of the wonderful ways God blesses us. It also reminds us to say thank you to our family and friends and people who do kind things for us.

Jesus, thank You for all the things You do to make me happy.

Jesus makes me happy.

Jesus Loves Me

Most importantly, love each other deeply.

1 Peter 4:8

D o you like it when someone tells you they love you? How do you feel when they give you a hug? Does it make you feel good? Jesus wants us to love others. He likes it when we say, "I love you." Jesus likes it when we show others that we love them. He likes it when we give people hugs or do something nice for them. We feel special because Jesus loves us. We can make other people feel special when we love them.

Jesus, thank You for loving me and making me feel special.

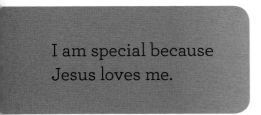

I am special because Jesus loves me.

Phil Waldrep, Phil Waldrep Ministries, Decatur, AL

God's Special Gift

Thanks be to God for his gift that is
too wonderful to explain.

2 Corinthians 9:15

Everybody likes to get gifts. Sometimes we
get gifts for our birthday or Christmas. Have
you ever asked for a special gift? If you got the
thing you wanted, were you surprised? Did you
know that God gave us a gift that is better than
any gift someone can give us? He gave us His Son,
Jesus. God did not have to send His Son. He did it
because He loves us! Jesus is God's very special
gift to us.

God, thank You for sending Your Son,
Jesus, to be my friend.

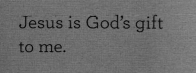

Jesus is God's gift
to me.

Thank You, God

Always give thanks to God the
Father for everything.

Ephesians 5:20

Have you tried to thank God for everything?
Have you told Him thank You for your mom
and dad? Have you told Him thank You for your
friends? God likes it when you tell Him thank You
for your clothes and for your shoes. He even likes
for you to thank Him for your dog or cat!

Everything we have comes from God. He gives
us things because He loves us. All He wants us to
do is say thank You for the things He gives
us. Have you thanked Jesus today?

Jesus, thank You for everything I have.

Jesus gives me so
many things.

Jesus Is with Me

God, we thank you. We thank you because you are near. We tell about the wonderful things you do.

Psalm 75:1

D o you sometimes feel alone? Are you sometimes scared at night? You do not have to be afraid, because you are never alone! God is everywhere. He is in your room at home. He is with you at school. God is even with you when you go to the doctor! Anyplace you go, God is there! And He will never leave you alone for one moment.

Jesus, thank You for being with me everywhere I go.

Jesus is always with me.

How Do I Pray?

Lord, please teach us how to pray, too.

Luke 11:1

One day when Jesus was praying, His friends asked Him to teach them to pray. Jesus said to them, "When you pray, say: 'Father, we pray that Your name will always be kept holy. We pray that Your kingdom will come. Give us the food we need for each day. Forgive us the sins we have done, because we forgive every person who has done wrong to us. And do not cause us to be tested'" (Luke 11:2–4). Jesus is our friend, and we can pray like this too.

Jesus, thank You for teaching me how to pray.

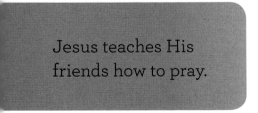

Jesus teaches His friends how to pray.

David Edwards, Author, Speaker, David Edwards Productions, Inc., Oklahoma City, OK www.davetown.com

Remember to Forgive

"When you are praying, and you remember that you are angry with another person about something, then forgive him."

Mark 11:25

S ometimes people are mean to us or things happen that are unfair. It can make us mad. We can feel so mad that we go around mad all day. It is a good thing that Jesus reminds us to forgive when we pray. Sometimes we cannot get rid of this anger by ourselves, but when we pray, Jesus can help us forgive.

Jesus, please help me forgive anyone who has been mean to me and help me forgive anything that has been unfair.

Remember that forgiveness is a choice.

God Will Hear Your Prayer

You will pray to him, and he will hear you.

Job 22:27

Our scripture today comes from the book of Job. Job had many bad things happen to him, and one of his friends told him this truth about God: "You will pray to him, and he will hear you." Job's friend was right. God heard Job's prayers. It is a promise from God that when we pray to Him, He will hear us. No matter where we are and no matter what is happening, God will hear our prayers. There are no troubles big enough to separate us from God.

God, thank You for hearing my prayers.

When you pray to God, He will hear you.

The Lord Is Close

The Lord is close to everyone who prays to him.

Psalm 145:18

T he book of Psalms is sometimes called the prayer book of the Bible. It is a great place to learn how to pray. King David wrote this psalm. David started out as a shepherd boy, and he believed that God was always close to him. God is always close to us too. God will be with us, no matter what happens to us. God is close to us when we pray.

God, thank You for being close to me when I pray to You.

God is always close to me.

David Edwards, Author, Speaker, David Edwards Productions, Inc., Oklahoma City, OK www.davetown.com

Praying for All God's People

Always pray for all God's people.
Ephesians 6:18

When we are little, sometimes we think that the prayers of grown-ups are better than ours. God does not think that way. For God, every person's prayers are important. Prayers change things. That is why the apostle Paul asked his friends the Ephesians to "always pray for all God's people." We can do this too. We can remember that every time we pray, we should pray for all God's people.

Jesus, please bless and care for all of Your people.

God loves to hear us pray. We can pray for all God's people.

David Edwards, Author, Speaker, David Edwards Productions, Inc., Oklahoma City, OK www.davetown.com

Trust God

Do not worry about anything. But pray and ask God for everything you need.

Philippians 4:6

The apostle Paul's words remind us not to worry and to ask God for what we need. This is good to do. We can also ask God for things we want. But sometimes we get mixed up about what we need and what we want. And then we can worry when do not get the things we want. Remember that God loves us and He will take care of us. He will give you what you need, and He wants to bless you with good things.

Jesus, thank You for taking care of me.

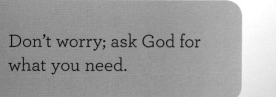

Don't worry; ask God for what you need.

It Is Nice to Say Thank You

Thank the Lord because he is good.
Psalm 106:1

The Bible says that God is good, and everything He does is good. We should thank Him for all the wonderful things in our lives. It is nice to say thank you, isn't it? We can say thank you for our warm beds and for the yummy food we eat. We can say thank you for our toys and the things we play with. We can say thank you for loving us and watching over us. Say thank you to the Lord Jesus because He is so good.

Jesus, thank You for being so good to us all the time and for loving us so much.

God is good. I can thank Him every day.

Sing Praises to God

I will praise the Lord all my life. I
will sing praises to my God as long
as I live.

Psalm 146:2

D o you love to sing? What is your favorite song
to sing? Can you sing it now? Jesus loves to
hear us sing songs about Him and to Him. Do you
know the song that goes, "Jesus loves me, this I
know, for the Bible tells me so"? The Bible tells us
to sing songs like this to show Jesus how much we
love Him. Sing a song to Jesus today!

Jesus, thank You for letting me sing songs to You. I want
to sing for You to let You know how much I love You.

I can show God how much I
love Him by singing to Him.

Praise the Lord

Let everything that breathes praise
the Lord.

Psalm 150:6

It is fun to be outside. You can see lots of wonderful animals doing all kinds of things. Birds fly high up in the sky and whistle and chirp. Squirrels play in the trees. Bees buzz around flowers.

God made everything we see. When we hear dogs barking, cats meowing, birds chirping, and people talking, we can always remember that God made us and all the animals. Listen to yourself breathe in and out! Isn't that wonderful? Thank God that He made you and gave you life.

Jesus, we praise You because you made us.

God gives us breath
and life.

Dr. Don Wilton, First Baptist Church, Spartanburg, SC

The Lord Is Great

Sing praise to the Lord, because he has done great things.

Isaiah 12:5

Did you know that the Lord Jesus wants us to sing and thank Him for the wonderful things He has done? He made the world and everything in it. He came to earth to save us and to show us how much God loves us. He has given us eyes to see, ears to hear, and legs to walk. Can you name some of His amazing blessings?

Jesus, thank You for everything You have done for me.

Jesus has done great things for me.

Feeling Yucky

I will praise the Lord at all times.
Psalm 34:1

Do you ever feel yucky? Maybe you feel sick or sad in your heart. Maybe you said something unkind to your friend, and now you feel sad. Do you feel sad when you have to go to bed and don't want to? You may feel yucky when you have to eat food you don't like. You can talk to Jesus when you are feeling yucky. He will listen to you.

The Bible tells us to thank the Lord always, no matter how yucky we feel or how bad things may be.

Jesus, help me to thank you always, even when I feel yucky.

Jesus understands when I feel yucky.

My Very Best

I will praise you, Lord, with all my heart.

Psalm 9:1

Do you love to run? I am sure you do. When I was a little boy, I would run and run all around the house. When I was playing outside, I would run as fast as I could. I ran with all my heart. That means I did my very best. Sometimes, after I had run a lot, I panted like a little dog, and my tongue stuck out! Isn't that funny?

Jesus wants you to tell Him how much you love Him. He wants you to praise Him and thank Him the very best you can.

Jesus, I will do my best to love You with all of my heart.

Jesus wants us to love Him the most.

God Is Creator

It is by faith we understand that the whole world was made by God's command.

Hebrews 11:3

Do you like to create and build things with Legos or Play-Doh? The Bible says in Genesis that God created everything. He created the light, day, night, stars, moon, water, land, trees, plants, fish, bears, lions, kangaroos, and people. Our God is an awesome Creator who made the whole world. He created you because He wants to be with you. He loves you and wants you to love and obey Him.

Dear God, You are an amazing Creator. Thank You for creating everything and for making me and loving me.

Believe that God created you and loves you. He wants you to love and obey Him.

Stephanie Perdue, Second Baptist Church, Warner Robins, GA

God Is Real

Faith means being sure of the things we hope for. And faith means knowing that something is real even if we do not see it.

Hebrews 11:1

G od created things we see and things we cannot see. God is real, even though we cannot see, hear, or touch Him. When you go outside on a breezy day, what is it that blows the trees and flowers? It is the wind. We cannot see or hold the wind, but we know it is there. By faith, we can know that God is real and that He loves us.

Dear God, help me have faith. I want to believe in You and obey You in all things.

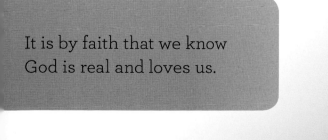

It is by faith that we know God is real and loves us.

God Can Do Big Things

"If your faith is as big as a mustard seed. . . . All things will be possible for you."

Matthew 17:20

Jesus was talking to His disciples. He wanted them to have faith in His power. He told them to have the faith of a mustard seed. Have you ever seen a mustard seed? It is one of the smallest seeds. It is so small you can barely see it, but when it is planted, the plant that comes from it can grow to be nine feet tall. This is a reminder that even if our faith is small, God can do big things through us.

Lord, please help me remember that with Your help anything is possible.

Even if our faith is small, God can do big things.

God Is Strong

Be careful. Continue strong in the faith. Have courage, and be strong. Do everything in love.

1 Corinthians 16:13–14

Jesus is God's Son. God sent Him to earth so He could make a way for you to know Him and love Him. When you believe in Him, it is called faith. God wants you to continue to believe even when it is not easy. This will take courage, and you will need to be strong. But God will always be there with you to help you.

Dear God, thank You for loving me and taking care of me. Help me have courage all the time.

We can trust God to take care of us.

Stephanie Perdue, Second Baptist Church, Warner Robins, GA

God Is Powerful

Jesus got up and gave a command to the wind and the waves. The wind stopped, and the lake became calm. Jesus said to his followers, "Where is your faith?"

Luke 8:24–25

Jesus was in a boat with His disciples on the Sea of Galilee. He was asleep when a big storm came. The men were very scared. Jesus spoke and calmed the storm with His voice. Just like the disciples, some things in life may make you afraid. But if you believe that Jesus is with you, you do not have to be scared.

Jesus, thank You for being in control of my life. I praise You for Your help when I need You.

Jesus is in control of everything.

Stephanie Perdue, Second Baptist Church, Warner Robins, GA

God Is Faithful

Be strong in the faith, just as
you were taught. And always be
thankful.

Colossians 2:7

Have you ever sung the song that goes, "My
God is so big, so strong and so mighty, there's
nothing my God cannot do"? Did you know that
you can be strong too? God is strong and mighty,
and He can help you be strong too. God wants you
to be strong in your faith. Your faith will grow when
you read His Word, pray, and listen to your parents
and teachers.

Dear God, help me read Your Word
and pray so that my faith will grow
bigger and stronger.

We can be strong
because God is strong
and mighty.

Jesus Is Kind and Strong

Jesus felt sorry for the blind men.
He touched their eyes, and at once
they were able to see.

Matthew 20:34

J esus was walking down the road. Two blind
men heard Jesus was nearby, so they shouted
to Him for help. Some people told the blind men
to be quiet, but they got even louder. They needed
Jesus' help so badly that they would not be quiet!
Jesus came over to them and asked what their
problem was. They told Him they were blind.
Jesus was kind enough to
touch them, and that very
second they could see!

Dear Lord, thank You for
caring about me. Help me call
out to You when I need You.

Pray to Jesus because
He is kind and strong!

Jesus Shares with Others

Jesus said, "Bring the bread and the fish to me."

Matthew 14:18

Big crowds of people came to hear Jesus teach. One day, about five thousand men came, plus their wives and kids. After a while, they got hungry for lunch. No one had any food except for one small boy, who had five pieces of bread and two small fish (see John 6:9). Jesus took the food and said a prayer. It was a miracle! There was enough food for all to eat. Jesus shared the food with everyone!

Dear Jesus, You are so powerful. Thank You for taking the little that I have and using it make a big difference.

Share what you have with others.

Rev. Jeremy Morton, Cartersville First Baptist Church, Cartersville, GA

Jesus Stops a Storm

Jesus stood up and commanded the wind and the waves to stop. He said, "Quiet! Be still!"

Mark 4:39

One night, Jesus' disciples were sailing in a boat. It started raining hard and got very windy. Waves were crashing into the boat. The disciples were very scared. But Jesus was not scared. He was asleep inside the boat. They woke Him up and asked for help. Jesus stood up and commanded the waves to be calm. No more wind and rain! It was smooth sailing.

Dear God, help me call on You when I am afraid. Help me always trust You.

When you are scared, call on Jesus. He loves you!

Rev. Jeremy Morton, Cartersville First Baptist Church, Cartersville, GA

Jesus Can Make Us Well

"[Jesus] makes the deaf hear! And those who can't talk—Jesus makes them able to speak."

Mark 7:37

Jesus was out walking. He saw a sad man in a crowd of people. The man could not hear and he could not talk. His friends asked Jesus for help. Jesus took a good look at the man. He touched his face and asked God to heal him. That very moment, the man was able to hear and speak! The whole crowd cheered because of Jesus' power.

Dear Lord, thank You that You can do anything! Help me love You with all my heart.

Jesus can make you well!

Take Your Friends to Jesus

Some people came, bringing a paralyzed man to Jesus.

Mark 2:3

One day Jesus was teaching inside a house. Four men came to the home carrying their sick friend on a mat. The man was lying on the mat because he could not walk. The house was very crowded, and the men could not get inside. Many people wanted to hear Jesus. So the four friends cut a hole in the roof and lowered the sick man down to Jesus. Jesus was very happy with their faith. He healed the sick man and made him walk again!

Dear Jesus, teach us to love our friends and care about their needs. Thank You for Your kindness to us.

Always help your friends find their way to Jesus.

Jesus Loves Children

"Let the little children come to me.
Don't stop them. The kingdom of
God belongs to people who are like
these little children."

Mark 10:14

People followed Jesus everywhere He went. He was a wonderful teacher. One day a big crowd came near Jesus. Parents were asking Him to bless their kids. So many kids were around, it made the disciples uncomfortable. They told the people to stop bringing their children to Jesus. But Jesus said, "No way. Let the kids come to Me. I love them all. Heaven is for people who love little children."

Dear God, thank You for loving me. Help me love You more every day. Thank You for accepting me just the way I am.

Jesus loves kids! They are important to Him!

Rev. Jeremy Morton, Cartersville First Baptist Church, Cartersville, GA

Obeying Makes Me Happy

"Now, my children, listen to me. Those who follow my ways are happy."

Proverbs 8:32

God tells us in His special book, the Bible, the things He wants us to do. When God says, "Follow My ways," He means we should obey Him. We learn His ways when we read the Bible and listen to what our parents and teachers tell us about Him.

God loves you. He wants you to be happy. He knows what is best for you. When you do the things He tells you to do, you will be happy.

Dear God, thank You for loving me. I want to be happy. Help me obey Your Word.

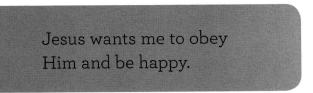

Jesus wants me to obey Him and be happy.

Dennis Nunn, Every Believer a Witness Ministries, Dallas, GA

I Love You, Jesus

"If you love me, you will do the things I command."

John 14:15

D o you know the song, "Jesus Loves Me"? If you do, sing it now. Jesus showed how much He loves us when He paid for our sins (all the bad things we do) on the cross. Jesus wants us to love Him too. It is good to tell Jesus that we love Him, but the Bible says we can show that we love Him by obeying Him.

Dear Jesus, thank You for loving me. Help me show You how much I love You by doing the things You tell me to do.

Jesus loves me, and He wants me to love Him.

How to Please God

Children, obey your parents in all things. This pleases the Lord.

Colossians 3:20

D o you love your mom and your dad? Of course you do! The Bible tells children to obey their parents, not just when they want to obey, but always. How do you act when your parents tell you to pick up your clothes, do your homework, or get ready for bed? Do you whine or fuss? Or do you say, "Yes, sir" or "Yes, ma'am" and do what they ask? God is pleased when you obey.

Dear Jesus, thank You for my parents. Help me obey them, even if I do not want to.

Jesus is happy when I obey my parents.

Young Children Can Obey God

Josiah was eight years old when he
became king. . . . He did what the
Lord said was right.

2 Chronicles 34:1–2

Josiah was only eight years old when God
made him a king. It was a very important job,
especially for a child! The Bible says that Josiah
loved the Lord and obeyed all His teachings. But
Josiah did what was right. How old are you? You
are never too young or too old to obey God and do
what is right.

Dear Jesus, I want to do what is right. Help me treat
other people right and always obey You.

No matter how old I
am, I want to obey.

How to Show
I Love Jesus

Even a child is known by his
behavior.

Proverbs 20:11

When we watch videos or television, we can usually tell who the good people are. Good people obey the law. Good people are kind to others. Can you think of someone in one of your favorite videos who is good?

God sees how we behave. People do too. God wants children to obey and be nice to others. Can you think of a time when you obeyed your parents today? Were you kind to someone today? We show the goodness of God when we are good.

Dear Jesus, help me always obey my parents and be kind to everyone.

Others see when I am kind
and good.

Obeying My Parents Is Important

Children, obey your parents the way the Lord wants.

Ephesians 6:1

Think about a cold winter day. When you get ready for school, your mom says, "Wear a warm coat." When you are eating breakfast, she says it again: "Wear a warm coat today." She tells you more than once because she knows it is important. When God tells us something more than one time, it is really important. God says again and again that He wants children to obey their parents. Listen to God and obey.

Dear God, I am glad You know what is best for me. I want to do what You say and obey my parents.

It is important for me to obey my parents.

Meet Grace

Let us, then, feel free to come before
God's throne. Here there is grace.
Hebrews 4:16

Grace had done a bad thing. She disobeyed her
mom and knew she was in big trouble. She
was scared! But she was in for a surprise. When
her mom came to tuck her in that night, they had
a serious talk about disobeying. Then, instead of
being punished, Grace's mom gave her a big hug
and a kiss and told her she loved her. Grace didn't
get what she deserved. Grace got grace!

Thank You, God, that You surprise me with grace. You
love me no matter what. I can talk to
You anytime, and I never have
to be afraid of You.

God shows me grace
every day.

Grace Is Free

The law was given through Moses, but grace and truth came through Jesus Christ.

John 1:17

Grace was a rule follower and always wanted to please her teacher. So when she could not make her art project look exactly like the teacher's sample, she became very upset. The teacher told her that she didn't have to do it just like she did. She never expected the students to do it perfectly. Once Grace understood that her drawing didn't have to be perfect, the project that had been no fun was a blast!

Thank You, God, for sending Jesus so that I do not have to be perfect. Thank You that Jesus is all I need.

Jesus is perfect so I do not have to be.

Debbie Schreve, First Baptist Church Texarkana, Texarkana, TX   291

Grace Is a Gift

I mean that you have been saved by grace because you believe. . . . It was a gift from God.

Ephesians 2:8

G race loved going to her grandmother's house for a lot of reasons. Grandma had her favorite snacks, played her favorite games, and always had a surprise gift just for her. Even though her grandmother had other grandkids she dearly loved, she always made Grace feel like she was the most special one . . . and that was the best gift of all! Grace's grandmother taught her about God's love. Grace knew that God thought she was special, just like her grandmother did.

Thank You, God, for Your gift of loving me and making me feel special. Help me love You more every day.

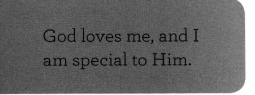

God loves me, and I am special to Him.

Debbie Schreve, First Baptist Church Texarkana, Texarkana, TX

Grace Is Special

Christ gave each one of us a special
gift.

Ephesians 4:7

G race had never liked her red hair and freckles.
Sometimes she got teased because of them.
Her mom always told her that these were special
gifts from God, but it wasn't until the Thanksgiving
play that she believed it. When the play called for
the lead character to be redheaded with freckles,
Grace got the part. Now, instead of wanting to be
like everyone else, Grace was thankful she was
different. The red hair and freckles God gave her
weren't so bad after all!

Thank You, God, that there is no one
exactly like me. I promise to use my special
gifts to help people learn about You.

I'm glad that God made
me just the way I am!

Grace Is Truthful

Grace teaches us to live on earth now in a wise and right way—a way that shows that we serve God.

Titus 2:12

Everyone in her class knew that Grace always chose Skittles first out of the candy basket at school. So when her teacher found a bag of Skittles on the floor, she put them on Grace's desk. Grace knew they weren't hers, but she really wanted them. She had a choice to make: keep them or give them back. Her teacher was very happy that Grace chose to tell the truth and give the candy back.

Thank You, God, for teaching me that it is always best to do the right thing. Others are watching, and I want to please You.

Doing the right thing makes God happy.

Grace Is
Never Lost

But God remembered Noah and all
the wild animals and tame animals
with him in the boat.

Genesis 8:1

Grace loved to spend time with her dad. Her favorite thing to do with him was to go shopping on Saturday mornings. One day, as her dad looked for a new fishing rod, Grace decided to trick him and hide in the center of a clothes rack. When she finally came out, she didn't see her dad anywhere and she got very scared. Suddenly she felt a hand on her shoulder and heard a familiar voice. Little did she know, her father had never taken his eyes off of her.

Thank You, God, that You always know where I am and never forget about me. I can always trust You!

God is always with me so I
am never alone.

Jesus Wants to Know Me

[Zacchaeus] ran ahead to a place where he knew Jesus would come. He climbed a sycamore tree so he could see Jesus.

Luke 19:4

Zacchaeus was so excited! Jesus was coming to town! He joined a large crowd of people and waited to see Jesus. Because he was not very tall, Zacchaeus decided to climb a tree so he could see Jesus for himself. When Jesus saw Zacchaeus, He told him to come down and take Him to his house. Jesus wanted to spend time with Zacchaeus, and He wants to spend time with you too!

Jesus, thank You for caring about me and wanting to spend time with me.

Jesus wants to be with me.

Dr. Lee Sheppard, Mabel White Baptist Church, Macon, GA

I Can Be a Helper

Then a Samaritan traveling down the road came to where the hurt man was lying.

Luke 10:33

The Samaritan was traveling down the road and found a man who had been beaten and robbed lying in the ditch. Even though the Samaritan did not know the man, he picked him up and took care of him. He bandaged his wounds, took him to an inn, and paid the innkeeper to take care of him. God wants us to help others who are in need. This is how we show His love to others.

Jesus, thank You for the opportunity to help others. Help me show Your love by helping others.

I can help others.

Getting Ready for the Storm

"The wise man built his house on rock."

Matthew 7:24

Are you afraid of storms? When the wind begins to blow, the thunder makes a loud crack, and the rain begins to fall, it can be frightening. When storms come, we have houses that give us shelter and keep us safe because our homes have a solid foundation. They are built on rock, not sand. Jesus is telling us that when bad things happen, we can trust Him. He is like a rock, and nothing can shake us when we put our trust in Him.

Jesus, thank You for being there for me and keeping me safe.

I can always trust Jesus to help me.

Listening to God

Mary was sitting at Jesus' feet and
listening to him teach.

Luke 10:39

This Mary was a friend of Jesus, and she loved to hear Him teach. She had never heard anyone teach like Jesus did. Even though Jesus was speaking to a crowd of people, she felt like He was speaking just to her. Did you know that Jesus speaks to us? He speaks to us when we read the Bible. He speaks to us when we pray. Sometimes He speaks to us through other people. When we listen, He speaks to us and tells us what we should do.

Jesus, thank You for speaking to me. Help me be a good listener.

Listen to what God says.

Dr. Lee Sheppard, Mabel White Baptist Church, Macon, GA

Why We Should Obey

[Jesus] said, "Throw your net into the water on the right side of the boat, and you will find some."

John 21:6

The disciples had fished all night and had not caught a single fish. They were tired and ready to go home. Jesus told them to throw their nets out one more time on the right side of the boat. The disciples said, "Lord, we have fished all night and caught nothing, but if You say to throw the nets in the water, we will." They did as Jesus said and caught so many fish, the boat almost sank. We should always obey God. He always knows what is best for us.

Jesus, help me be obedient to You.

Always obey Jesus.

Dr. Lee Sheppard, Mabel White Baptist Church, Macon, GA

God Loves You

Then a voice came from heaven and
said, "You are my Son and I love
you. I am very pleased with you."
Luke 3:22

Jesus was baptized by John the Baptist in the
Jordan River. He wanted more than anything
to do what God wanted Him to do. God loves Jesus
very much, and He was so pleased with Jesus that
He let everyone hear Him tell Jesus how much He
loved Him.

God loves you so much! When you are His child,
there is nothing you can do that will cause Him not
to love you. He is looking down from
heaven and is very pleased when
we do His will.

Jesus, thank You for loving me
and watching over me. Help me do
Your will.

God loves me for who I am.

Don't Be Afraid

The angel said to her, "Don't be afraid, Mary. . . . You will give birth to a son, and you will name him Jesus."

Luke 1:30–31

God sent His angel to tell Mary about His plan for her life. She was going to have a baby, and that little boy was going to be the Son of God. Mary was so afraid! She loved God, but she did not understand what the angel was telling her. She did not know all of God's plans, but she was obedient and trusted God. You do not have to be afraid either because God is good. Trust God and obey Him.

Thank You, God, for sending Jesus so we can live with You forever.

When we trust God, we have no reason to be afraid.

Making Room for Jesus

There were no rooms left in the inn. So
she wrapped the baby with cloths and
laid him in a box where animals are fed.

Luke 2:7

Joseph and Mary had traveled a long way. Mary
was very tired when she and her husband
arrived at the little town of Bethlehem. Her baby
was going to be born at any moment! There was no
time to delay. But there were no empty rooms at the
inn. What would Mary do? They finally found an
animal barn where they could stay. Jesus was born,
and Mary dressed Him in some warm cloths and
laid Him in a feeding box.

Thank You, God, for taking good care of baby Jesus
and His parents. You are always watching over us. We never
have to be afraid!

God always watches over
His children.

Pastor Dusty & Mrs. Patsy McLemore,
Lindsay Lane Baptist Church, Athens, AL

Shepherds in the Field

That night, some shepherds were in the fields nearby watching their sheep.

Luke 2:8

God wanted everyone to know that He was sending His Son to be born in Bethlehem. Baby Jesus would be the Savior of the world! So God sent an angel to tell the shepherds the good news of Jesus' birth. They were so excited! The Savior had come! Angels do not sing to us from the sky. But we have the Bible to read so we can learn all about Jesus whenever we want to.

Thank You, God, for the Bible. It helps us know Jesus better and love Him more.

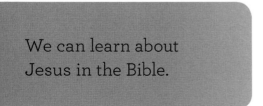

We can learn about Jesus in the Bible.

Pastor Dusty & Mrs. Patsy McLemore,
Lindsay Lane Baptist Church, Athens, AL

Listen, Everyone: A King Is Born

So the shepherds went quickly and found Mary and Joseph.

Luke 2:16

The shepherds had never heard anything like this before. This was a very special night. The stars were shining bright, and the angels were singing! They were praising God! The angels told the shepherds to go to Bethlehem and look for Mary and Joseph. Their baby was about to be born, and they were to call Him Jesus. This child would be born a King. And not just any king, but the King of all kings!

Dear Jesus, I am so glad You were born a King! Thank You, God, for our special gift of King Jesus!

God's special gift to us was a King!

What Makes You Happy?

When the wise men saw the star, they were filled with joy.

Matthew 2:10

Wise men traveled from far away. They saw a star in the sky and knew it was there for a reason. God created all the stars, but this star was special. The wise men wondered where the star was leading them. When they got to Bethlehem, they knew! This bright star had led them straight to Jesus. When they saw the baby boy, their hearts were filled with joy. Jesus is still filling hearts with joy even today.

Dear Jesus, You are the light of the world. Thank You for leading us and giving us joy.

Real joy comes from talking with Jesus.

How to Make God Smile

The little child began to grow up.
He became stronger and wiser, and
God's blessings were with him.

Luke 2:40

The Bible teaches us how to eat and drink to be healthy. Being healthy makes us grow strong and wise. Jesus was born a child just like us. So He knew if He was going to be able to serve God, He must grow strong and learn. It was very important to Jesus to receive God's blessings. Jesus began to talk to God in prayer. He also listened to God. God loves when we talk to Him. Prayer makes God smile. Do you want to make God smile? Jesus did!

Dear God, thank You for hearing my prayers. Help me hear You speak to me.

> When we make God smile, we make others smile too.

Pastor Dusty & Mrs. Patsy McLemore,
Lindsay Lane Baptist Church, Athens, AL

Remember This

Train a child how to live the right way. Then even when he is old, he will still live that way.

Proverbs 22:6

Your parents teach you about Jesus because they want you to know Him and love Him. Jesus wants you to grow up and remember what your parents and teachers have taught you about Him. He also wants you to remember what you read about Him in the Bible. Jesus said if we love Him, we will obey His rules. Your parents teach you about Jesus so that you will always love Him and trust Him. You can always have Jesus as your very best friend, even when you grow old!

Dear Jesus, I want to learn everything about You so I can be more like You. Will You help me remember to learn about You and obey You today?

If you love Jesus, you will obey Jesus every day.

Rev. Chuck Allen, Sugar Hill Church, Sugar Hill, GA

All in the Family

"As for me and my family, we will serve the Lord."

Joshua 24:15

One of God's gifts to us is our family. We have family who live with us, a family of friends, and a family at church. God wants you and all your family to serve Him. Can you think of something your whole family can do to serve God? Maybe you can all collect food to give to people who are hungry. Maybe you can work together at a shelter where people live who do not have homes of their own. When we serve other people, we are acting like Jesus. You can serve the Lord by helping somebody today.

Dear Jesus, thank You for my friends and my family. I want to serve You by helping somebody. Help me know who to help and how to help them.

Serving the Lord means helping other people.

I Am a Special Gift

Grandchildren are the reward of old people.

Proverbs 17:6

Old people love their grandchildren because they make them feel young. God has a special way to make old people feel happy. He gives them grandchildren, just like you. Grandparents pinch your cheeks and show people your pictures and love you so much because you are their very special gift from God. God does not just love you when you are young. He never stops loving you.

Dear God, thank You for making me a special gift to my grandparents. Please tell my grandparents that You love them, and I will too.

You are a reward from God.

Believe in the Lord

They said to him, "Believe in the Lord Jesus and you will be saved—you and all the people in your house."

Acts 16:31

Do you know people in your family who do not believe in Jesus? Do you have friends who do not know who Jesus is? God wants everyone to love Him. You can pray and ask God to help you show His love to your friends and family. You can tell people about Jesus and how much He loves them. You can do kind things for them and be an example of God's love. Look for ways to share the love of Jesus to everyone around you so that they can know about Jesus.

Dear Jesus, thank You for loving me so much. Help me show others how much You love them.

Believe in Jesus and you will be with Him forever.

Love and Honor

"Honor your father and your mother."
Exodus 20:12

God is your heavenly Father, and He loves you very much. He knew that you needed someone to watch over you and take care of you, so He gave you a mom and a dad to love you. When God tells you to honor your mom and dad, He is saying that He wants you to love them and obey them. You should listen to them and do what they ask you to do because they know what is best for you. You should use kind words and look for ways to help them. You show God that you love Him when you obey and are kind to your parents. Thank God for your mom and dad, and thank them for all they do for you.

Dear God, please help me obey my mom and dad so that I can honor them. Thank You for my mom and dad. They are very special gifts from You.

To honor someone is to love them.

Rev. Chuck Allen, Sugar Hill Church, Sugar Hill, GA

Follow the Leader

A wise son takes his father's advice.

Proverbs 13:1

A wise person is someone who knows the difference between good and bad and chooses to be good. Your dad wants to help you make good choices. God gave you a dad so that you can learn from him. Have you ever played "Follow the Leader"? You should listen to what your dad has to say and follow his lead. That is what God wants you to do. Jesus did what His Father, God, asked Him to do. You should follow Jesus' example and follow God and your dad.

Dear Jesus, thank You for showing me how to follow the leader. Help my dad teach me the difference between good and bad. And help me always choose to be good.

Being wise is choosing to be good and not bad, just like Jesus.

Contributors

Scripture Index